THE OTHER MRS. WATSON

Who was the elusive second wife of John Watson, trusted friend and chronicler of the great Sherlock Holmes? The secret is now revealed in *The Other Mrs. Watson*, eight stories featuring Amelia Watson, devoted and opinionated wife of the good doctor, and intrepid (if a bit reluctant) amateur sleuth. Jack the Ripper is back, and up to his old tricks . . . Ghosts and demons materialise to trouble the living . . . An old acquaintance of Holmes's reappears, with cut-throats on her tail . . . And murder seems to lurk around every corner!

MICHAEL MALLORY

◆

THE OTHER MRS. WATSON

Complete and Unabridged

LINFORD
Leicester

First published in Great Britain

First Linford Edition
published 2016

A catalogue record for this book is available
from the British Library.

ISBN 978–1–4448–2808–5

Published by
F. A. Thorpe (Publishing)
Anstey, Leicestershire

Set by Words & Graphics Ltd.
Anstey, Leicestershire
Printed and bound in Great Britain by
T. J. International Ltd., Padstow, Cornwall

This book is printed on acid-free paper

I find from my notebook that it was January, 1903, just after the conclusion of the Boer War . . . The good Watson had at that time deserted me for a wife, the only selfish action which I can recall in our association.

Mr. Sherlock Holmes, from
'The Adventure of the
Blanched Soldier'
by A. Conan Doyle

Contents

The Adventure of the Left-Behind Wife

Letter to Mrs. Elizabeth Newington
from Mrs. Amelia Watson
July 19, 1903

My dearest Beth —
Forgive me for not having returned your correspondence until now, but John was ill recently. Nothing serious, but for a medical man he takes notoriously little care of himself, and he should really know better than to stay up the entire evening hidden in a hedge, playing out some *Boy's Own* detective adventure yet again. Yes, Beth, I am afraid that I must report that the 'boys' are at it again, John and that demented friend of his. I tell John that he is entirely too old for this sort of nonsense — fifty-one on his next birthday — but he does not listen. Why should he, after all? I am only his wife; and, as he so frequently points out to me, merely a *woman*. I begin to fear, Beth, that he has

3

clung to that prig Holmes for so long, and has had his ego punctured so often by this same companion of choice, that he can only justify his manhood by putting me in my place as 'merely a woman'.

Yet I hope I do not sound unduly harsh towards John. He really can be a dear; kind and warm-hearted, as you well know, and all too willing to do a worthy deed for any needy person who cannot pay (if it were not for his Army pension, Beth, I should probably have to scrub floors to support us). And I have great reason to feel soft towards him at present — but more of that later.

What I really want to tell you is that I have finally met the 'great man' himself. Prior to this I have known him only through John's magazine stories, which tend to colour reality in hues that would have embarrassed Oscar Wilde's tailor, and through his incessant speaking of him. It is 'Holmes, Holmes, Holmes' all day long and into the evening, as if no one else exists. But I begin to digress. Let me tell you of the singular (to use John's favourite word) events that led up to my meeting the world's foremost consulting detective, Mr. Sherlock Holmes.

(And Beth, be honest — have you ever known anyone else on earth named *Sherlock*?)

How would John put it? Let's see . . .

It was on a bleak grey morning in the spring of the year when London was in the grip of a persistent, many-tentacled fog (how am I doing so far, dear?) that I first saw the old match-selling woman.

That morning my husband, Dr. John H. Watson, had no sooner sat down to breakfast in our small but comfortable flat when a rather grimy youth appeared at the door, message in hand. A message for John delivered in such fashion means one of two things: he is required immediately for a medical emergency, or the game is once more afoot. Alas, it was the latter.

The change that comes over him whenever he reads a summons from his friend, Mr. Sherlock Holmes, is quite remarkable. He loses all appetite immediately, leaps up from the table, and begins prancing around with great agitation. His eyes take on new light; and while some may think me mad for saying so, I swear that the grey in his hair actually streaks back to its natural brown and he becomes once again a callow youth wild for adventure.

'Holmes needs me, my dear,' he said excitedly, racing to his desk and burrowing through the files heaped upon it until he had found his Bradshaw's. 'Please believe me, Beth, that my heart sinks at the very sight of that railway timetable.

'You are not leaving town, again?' I asked plaintively, to which he replied, 'I am very sorry, my dear, but this is something urgent. That was Holmes's very word, *urgent*.' Opening a desk drawer, John withdrew his old service revolver.

'John!'

'Hmm? Oh, don't worry, Amelia, I do not expect to have to use this. I carry it because . . . well, I carry it because I feel almost like I am missing a limb without it. I suppose you could call it a habit.'

Two grown men, two habits: one injects himself with cocaine, while the other plays with guns. I tell you, Beth, it is a wonder they are both still alive.

The most distressing act was when he pulled down his battered suitcase and began throwing clean shirts into it, a week's worth at least, ruining whatever press they might once have possessed.

'Oh, John, how long will you be gone this time?'

'I cannot say, my dear, but I shall write to you. Do not worry, my love. I shall be fine.' Yes, *he* would be fine.

Throwing his hat on — backwards — he raced for the stairs and I followed. 'What if a patient comes?'

'Refer them to Dr. Fennyman, as usual. Goodbye, my dear.' And out he went.

Do you know, Beth, that last month we actually received a thank-you note from Dr. Fennyman, so improved has his practice become because of John running off with Holmes?

Once again left to finish breakfast alone, I tried to read the *Times*, but it meant nothing. Words are only words if you cannot concentrate on the idea behind them, and at that moment the only thing I could concentrate on was the loss of my husband to a misanthropic mistress named Sherlock Holmes.

But I had not long to wait before the adventure began.

Deciding to take a stroll along the street (however gloomy it was outside, it was gloomier still in the quiet flat) and perhaps get in a bit of shopping, I bundled up against the misty chill and went out. I had not even set foot on the pavement when I saw her.

Do you remember, Beth, back in the theatre there was a fellow who played nothing but walk-ons, spear-carriers or townspeople, rarely ever getting the chance to read a line? I cannot recall his name, but I am sure you will remember him, because we used to make such fun of his ability to be seen. No matter how insignificant his role, and no matter how vital it was that he blend into a crowd, this fellow would stand out by his too-careful attempt to appear inconsequential; rather than being a part of a crowd, he acted the role of a man who was a part of a crowd, and stood out like a black eye. Thus it was with this woman.

She was old and bent, and appeared to be the proprietress of a match booth, but there was something about her which was not right. In trying to become a part of the street she fussed and fidgeted and did any number of old-womanly things, all of which appeared to my eyes to be a little too carefully rehearsed. However, figuring that this was her selling technique, making herself just a bit older and feebler than she actually was to gain additional buyer sympathy, I gave the crone no more thought and went about my business.

I shall not bore you with the details of my expedition, except to say that nothing in the shops suited me that day. I was just starting the journey home when I saw her again, standing at the corner near the shop, advertising her wares in a flat, shrill, sing-song voice and blessing the few who actually passed a halfpenny her way. My immediate reaction was that this strange woman had followed me, yet why on earth would she do so? Could I simply be imagining things? Or had I let the perpetual talk of mystery and mayhem that flurries around our home like winter's snow melt into my head?

Paying no attention to the woman — who indeed, seemed to pay no attention to me — I made my way back and did not encounter her again.

The evening was long and sleepless, as it usually is when John is off playing, and I awoke the next morning in a poor mood, uncomfortable and not a little bit angry. How dare he keep running off at a moment's notice with no consideration for me, and little for the patients who have come to depend upon him!

The morning's post brought his promised letter, but I waited before opening it, letting myself cool down somewhat. As usually happens, the anger subsided and gave way to the dull ache of loneliness. I married John because I wanted to be with him, and I presumed that he wanted to be with me as well.

His note placed him at Henley-on-Thames, of all places, and said very little else except that his new 'mission' was a vital one and that he missed my presence. Oh, John . . . dear, sweet, guileless John . . .

I had already decided to venture forth that day, having found nothing within the flat to keep me occupied for another solitary afternoon, and glanced out of the window to check the weather. Immediately I saw that she was back, the old match-seller. Only this time, I caught her looking directly at our window, just for the tiniest fleeting moment. Whoever this woman was, and whatever her purpose, I was now convinced that she was watching me.

As you well know, Beth, I am not a person who is easily rattled or whose nerves are close to the surface; but this strange haggard woman, dressed in black rags, innocuously peddling her matches while keeping a close watch of my movements, unnerved me greatly. I cancelled all plans to leave the premises and instead attempted to teach the game of chess to Missy, our new young maid, who looked upon the prospect of ceasing her duties for an afternoon of amusement as the greatest thing that had ever happened to her.

I remained inside the next day as well,

having received my daily dispatch from John — vague as usual, but a touch more affectionate — and I was quite relieved to notice that the old match-seller was nowhere to be seen from our window. My relief was short-lived, however, with the appearance of Missy in our chambers, an odd expression on her face.

'Ma'am, there is a woman here to see the doctor.'

'The doctor is away, I am afraid. Please give her the address of Dr. Fennyman.'

'Yes'm, I tried to do that, but she wouldn't listen. She says it's to be Dr. Watson or no one.'

Before I could speak to reply, 'It must be no one then,' another voice was heard outside the door — a shrill, high, wheezy voice.

'Doctor Watson did me a good turn onest, he did, soes it's Dr. Watson I wants ter see.'

The woman bustled her way in past Missy before either of us could object. Her tray of matches was gone, but she wore the same black ragged dress and shawl in which I had seen her the past two days. The woman coughed violently, then sank — nearly fell — into a chair.

'Get some water, Missy,' I called, and when she had left to fetch it I approached the woman and asked: 'What do you want with me?'

Blinking her bleary eyes as though trying to focus them, she wheezed: 'Wit you, dearie? Oh, I don't want nottin' wit you. It's Dr. Watson I want.'

As I came closer to her the entire plot suddenly became clear to me, as if a cloud had suddenly lifted and shown me the light. I say *plot*, because that is exactly what it was, Beth — a plot of the most devious sort. This woman, I now understood, had indeed been watching me, spying on me while John was away, and I was sure I knew why. When Missy returned with the water, I told her that the situation was well under control and sent her out.

'So, madam, it is Dr. Watson you want?' I said.

The old woman replied, 'Yes, dearie, it's him what I wants.'

'Well, I want him, too, Mr. Holmes!'

For the tiniest instant a look of total shock crossed the 'old woman's' face, then it was gone again. Coughing loudly, 'she' said: 'I don't knows whatcher mean.'

'Please, Mr. Holmes, do not insult my intelligence with this charade any longer. Tell me why you have sent my husband out of the city on some trumped-up cause so you can spy on me.'

Suddenly the figure's demeanour changed completely. Rather than slumping in the chair, the 'old woman' sat up stiffly, 'her' cold grey eyes boring into mine. But believe me, Beth, I stared back with every ounce of my being, refusing to be intimidated.

Finally 'she' said, 'Very well, madam,' in a much deeper, more resonant voice, and began to peel away the layers of the match-seller: first the shawl and long grey hair, then the sharp beakish nose complete with a wart, then the dress itself. Underneath was a man I knew to be roughly fifty, but looking older, gaunt with thinning dark hair, wearing a plain shirt and thin trousers, the bottoms of which were rolled up so as not to show underneath the dress. He kept the old woman's square shoes on his feet.

'May I smoke?' he asked curtly.

'Of course. Now please tell me what this is about, Mr. Holmes.'

'I will, but you must tell me something first,' he said, nervously lighting up a cigarette. 'How did you see through my disguise? Or was it just a lucky guess?'

I had such an urge at that moment to reply 'It was elementary,' but I managed to fight it down. 'It was no guess, Mr. Holmes,' I answered, 'but in truth I did not see through it at all; I smelled through it!'

'I beg your pardon?'

'Your skill at make-up is quite remarkable, it lives up to every report John has written about it.' Here he bowed his head slightly, acknowledging the compliment, and a small tight smile played on his lips. I went on: 'But it was still obviously make-up. Anyone who has ever encountered greasepaint, nose putty and spirit gum knows that nothing on earth smells like it. When I got close enough to you to detect the scent of the make-up, I wondered why an old woman would wear theatrical cosmetics in public. Why would anyone, for that matter? Then I realized that there was only one person in London who would do so.'

With a sudden movement Holmes banged himself on the forehead with the palm of his hand, spilling a good bit of ash on the furniture in the process. 'Ah! What a fool I was! Of course! Watson told me you had been in amateur theatrics.' So John had actually mentioned me to the great Sherlock Holmes! 'My congratulations on your successful deduction,' he mumbled.

'Now it is your turn, Mr. Holmes. Why have you gone through all this? Why have you taken my husband away from me?'

'Because I wanted to meet the woman who had taken him away from *me*,' he answered fiercely. 'My rival for his affections, as it were.'

At that moment, Beth, I did not know what to say. Of his complete sincerity there was no doubt, likewise his innocence; in his own way he loved my husband, though I doubt that word would have sprung to his mind. Immediately I saw the real Sherlock Holmes: an isolated and highly vulnerable man who had denied himself a good deal of what life had to offer in the pursuit of his profession, his 'duty', as it were, and a man who had but one friend in the world — only one. And here I stood as the force that threatened to remove that friend.

'Madam, I am lost without my Boswell, can you understand that?' Holmes cried.

'I can try to, Mr. Holmes. Does John know that our meeting is taking place?'

'No, of course not. He is quite comfortable at a country inn in Henley, watching the other guests like a hawk and reporting their every move to me. I have told him that a notorious international jewel thief is expected to pass through the area and have asked that he watch for any unusual comings and goings. He, in turn, thinks I am at Bray, doing likewise. When the affair is over, I shall have recovered the jewels. Here they are, as a matter of fact.' He reached into a pocket and brought out a dozen large and breathtaking gemstones. 'Yes, they are real; I captured the actual criminal last week. But at the end of this latest adventure, your good husband will have yet another exploit to write for the popular press, and will be the happier for it. So you see, madam, there is no harm done.'

'Do not keep him out too long,' I said, and with a subtle laugh by way of reply, the man was gone.

John came home a day later, exhilarated of course, and itching to sit down at his writing desk to compose the new tale. Once again, it was 'Holmes, Holmes, Holmes, Holmes, Holmes.' But at least I had the satisfaction this time of knowing, or at least sensing, that when the two are out on one of their 'games', Mr. Holmes is likewise treated to 'Amelia, Amelia, Amelia, Amelia . . . ' As I am sure my name will never appear in one of his fictions, I must content myself with that.

That would have been the end of the story, dear Beth, except for one last thing. Not a week later John was once again summoned by his friend, this time for lunch. I was not invited, of course. When John returned his expression was indescribable. I positively thought he was going to burst! He asked me to close my eyes and hold out my hand, and into it he placed a stunning, blue-white diamond, roughly the size of a sixpence!

'Where on earth did you get this?' I asked, and breathlessly, he explained that it was a reward for his and Holmes's capture of the jewel thief. Holmes had given it to him, he said, claiming that he had no use for it.

'Perhaps you should pass it on to your new wife, Watson,' he quoted Holmes as saying. 'Consider it a belated wedding present from yours truly.'

It is amazing what a stone of that size and beauty does towards establishing a forgiving mood. I am wearing it in a ring as I write this, and thinking of dear John out gallivanting around the countryside with his peculiar friend, keeping the world safe from crime and villainy, real or imagined, and awaiting his return.

I am afraid I must leave you now, Beth, as Missy has come in for our nightly chess game. And do you know — that the little snip actually *won* yesterday? Really!

My best to Robert.

Yours ever,

Amelia.

The Adventure of the Ripper's Scrawl

'John, I wish to leave immediately,' I said quietly but firmly.

'But my dear, we have only just arrived,' my husband replied.

'We have been at this dreadful party exactly fifty-three minutes, which has nothing to do with my wanting to leave.'

John smiled at another passing chorus of stuffed shirts with champagne glasses, then asked: 'Are you unwell?' This is invariably the first question from his lips whenever I speak a complaint of any kind — presumably the effect of so many years as a medical man.

'Physically, I have never been better, but I refuse to stay in the same room with that horrible man over there. The brute made overtures towards me!'

'The damnable cad! Which one is he?'

I levelled an accusatory finger at the villain, but upon spotting him the fiery indignation that had flared in John's eyes

23

quickly cooled. 'Amelia, that is Lord Wilby, Under-Secretary for Home Affairs,' he groaned.

'Who is now trying to negotiate an affair of his own,' I snapped back. 'I demand you defend my honour.'

'My dear, one cannot go about assailing a member of the government like Don Quixote charging the windmill.'

While normally the most considerate of men, there are still odd moments when John can be as infuriating as his misanthropic friend, Sherlock Holmes. I was about to tell him so when our host suddenly appeared.

'Is something the matter, Mrs. Watson? You look distressed,' said Sir Melville Macnaghten.

'It is nothing,' John replied before I could get a word out. 'My wife just remembered she . . . forgot to wind the clock. Is that not right, dear?'

'If you say so, darling,' I said coolly, while throwing him a glare that screamed: *We will speak more of this later*.

'I see,' our host said, obviously not convinced but polite enough to let the matter drop. Like John, Sir Melville Macnaghten was sturdily built and wore a moustache, though he was considerably shorter and nowhere near as handsome. The sum of my knowledge regarding him was that he was a career police official who had called upon John for professional assistance in the past, and who had just been appointed head of Scotland Yard's Criminal Investigation Department. This evening's *soirée* at his home in Chelsea was to celebrate the promotion.

'I'm very pleased you could come this evening,' Sir Melville was saying. 'I also invited your friend Holmes, though I did not receive a reply.'

'Mr. Holmes is not much of one for dinner parties,' I said, leaving unspoken the thought that in this instance, I did not blame him.

'Oh, it is nothing as simple as that, Mrs. Watson,' Sir Melville said. 'Holmes has not spoken to me for thirteen years.'

'Heavens, what did you do to him?'

A tiny smile broke out under his moustache. 'I had the temerity to solve the Ripper case.'

'Jack the Ripper?' I said. 'I thought that still unsolved.'

'Officially, it still is, due to the Vurczak business.'

I was now completely lost. 'Werjack? What is a werjack?'

'Not what, Mrs. Watson; who. Vurczak was an immigrant butcher living in the East End, who for a time was the Yard's leading suspect. He was later exonerated, but not before a neighbourhood mob, believing him to be the Ripper, hunted him down and killed him.'

'How awful,' I said.

'Yes, it was unsettling, to say the least,' Sir Melville acknowledged. 'But because of that incident I have never made public my case against the man I believe to be Jack the Ripper. Even though the man himself is now dead, his family remains vulnerable.'

'Sir Melville did, however, disclose his theory to Holmes and me,' John said, 'though Holmes took exception to his conclusions.'

'Quite strongly,' Sir Melville added. 'In the end he declared that the next time he spoke to me it would be to provide the Ripper's true identity, and since he has never come up with a suspect of his own he has not spoken to me since 1890.'

'He still remains convinced, though, that there is a secret message hidden inside that scrawl,' John said.

'What scrawl?' I asked, not because I particularly wanted to know, but because I hated being left out of a conversation.

'The Ripper left a message in chalk on a wall near two of the murder sites,' Sir Melville answered. 'It read: *The Juwes are not the men who will be blamed for nothing.*'

'What on earth does that mean?'

'No one knows. Equally puzzling was the fact that the word *Jews* was spelled J-U-W-E-S, which I'm told has Masonic significance.'

Given the ghastly direction this conversation had taken, I was not unhappy when it was interrupted by the sudden appearance in the room of a uniformed constable, who marched straight to Sir Melville and began whispering in his ear. I saw Sir Melville's face darken; and when the constable had finished he turned to me, taking my hand. 'Mrs. Watson, I am terribly sorry, but I need to borrow your husband. I am afraid we must leave at once.'

'What has happened?' John asked, and for an instant I saw the lightning flash of youthful excitement that comes over him whenever he is summoned by Holmes.

'I cannot explain now, but your medical expertise shall be of great use to me, Doctor. Mrs. Watson, would you be so good as to give my regrets to the rest of the guests? Say I was called away on official business.'

I started to protest, but Sir Melville cut me off with a clipped, 'Thank you,' and marched out of the room, taking my husband with him.

It was nearly two o'clock when John returned home. I was still awake, having been restlessly wandering through the pages of *Our Mutual Friend*. I had every intention of berating him for abandoning me at the party and forcing me to find my own way home. However, one look at him caused my anger to abate. Pale, exhausted and shaking, John had obviously had a much worse night than I. 'Would you mind telling me what that was all about?' was the best I could do.

'Murder, my dear,' John said softly. 'A man's body was found in an alleyway near Soho.'

'Dear God!'

'Oh, that is only the beginning. I knew the man. At least, I knew him years ago when he was a young medical student. Thedgehughes was his name. He was quite a brilliant student, but then something happened to him and he seemed to drop completely out of sight. I hadn't seen him since his training days at Bart's. Until tonight.'

'I'm so sorry, darling.'

'I haven't told you the worst yet, Amelia. The body had been . . . *ripped*. And on a nearby wall someone had written the scrawl.'

'The scrawl? John, you can't mean — '

'It was exactly the same as Sir Melville quoted, misspelt word for word.'

'What does it mean?'

John looked at me with eyes reddened

by fear and exhaustion. 'It means we brought him back, Amelia. Somehow, with all our talk of the Whitechapel murders last evening, we managed to resurrect Jack the Ripper.'

★   ★   ★

The next day's newspapers featured a full account of the horrible murder, including the fact that it was John who identified the body; yet the papers stopped short of linking the murder to Jack the Ripper. That would not happen for another week, when the body of a wealthy silk merchant, improbably named Galahad Arnaught, turned up near the docks. Hastily written across the pavement near the body was the scrawl. Still clinging to the irrational fear that he was somehow responsible, this second horror seemed to bother John even more than the first. But it was the third such killing, which was reported three days later, that seemed to cast him into a near-total state of despondency.

'The blood-drenched body of Sir Robert Blamefort was discovered in the early morning hours, near Seven Dials. His throat had been slashed; his abdomen was — '

'John, must you read that aloud?' I protested.

'Sorry,' he muttered, dropping the paper down on the floor next to his chair. Then with sudden and startling agitation, he cried: 'When will this terrible business end? What is the meaning of it all? Why are men of status being struck down instead of women of the streets?'

'John, you cannot seriously be arguing that the lives of the male aristocracy are worth more than women of the common classes.'

'No, no, no, of course not. It's just that . . . ' He stopped for a moment, struggling to find the right words. 'It is part of a pattern, Amelia; it has to be. The choice of seemingly unrelated victims, that damnable scrawl . . . it all adds up to *something*. But what am I doing to help discover the answer? *Nothing!* Why on earth hasn't Holmes contacted me?'

At long last I realized the source of

John's dark mood. A major crime spree was taking place, a puzzle of immense proportions, and he was being left out of the investigation.

Up to this point I had been secretly rejoicing in the silence coming from Baker Street, knowing that every time John returned to Holmes I was all but forgotten. On the other hand, a few lonely nights would still be preferable to watching him brood so. After carefully weighing the consequences, I suggested: 'Why don't you go to Mr. Holmes and find out?'

'Yes, yes, perhaps I should,' John said. 'I shall go at once.' He readied himself quickly, kissed me goodbye, and left.

I asked our maid Missy to put off her afternoon duties for a leisurely game of chess — something that required very little persuasion — but much to my surprise John was back in less than an hour, looking like he had witnessed the execution of his best friend.

'Now what is it?' I asked. 'Was Mr. Holmes gone?'

'Oh, no, he was there,' John said quietly

while staring at the floor. 'He turned me away.'

'The brute!'

'But he sent a message.'

'A message?'

'Yes, it seems he did not want to see me at all,' John said, sounding like a hurt child. 'He wants to see you, Amelia.'

★ ★ ★

I was ushered up to the hallowed rooms of 221b by Martha Hudson, Holmes's chatty, grey-haired landlady. 'He's in one of his moods, dear,' she whispered conspiratorially as we approached the door.

I knocked and received the barked reply: 'Come in, Mrs. Watson!'

My first thought upon entering was to race back out to tell Mrs. Hudson that her house was on fire, so thick was the smoke. But it turned out to be nothing more than the product of Holmes's overworked pipe.

'Could we please open a window?' I coughed.

33

'As you wish,' Holmes said impatiently, throwing open the window and letting some of the noxious cloud escape into Baker Street.

'Thank you. Now, Mr. Holmes, before I say anything else I must tell you that I do not appreciate your latest cavalier dismissal of John. He was positively crushed.'

'Watson knows me better than anyone, madam. He will get over it. But come, look at this.' He forcefully directed my attention through the smoky haze to a blackboard on which was written the scrawl of the Ripper, now horribly familiar.

'*This* is why you asked me up here?' I said. 'I would have thought that you would be out investigating these horrible murders instead of practising your handwriting.'

Holmes's luminous grey eyes pierced the acrid smoke like the fog lights of a coach. 'The police, it seems, have chosen not to invite me into their investigations, and there is very little a consulting detective can do if no one elects to consult him.'

At that instant I felt a touch of sympathy for him. Like John, he had been completely left out in the cold. No, that was not quite right. John had been involved in the discovery of the first victim. What a blow to Holmes's ego it must have been to read in the papers that his Boswell had been asked to assist in a murder case when he had not. That at least could explain the curt dismissal of his old friend.

'But that is of little consequence,' Holmes said, waving his hand, 'since I am convinced that this scrawl holds the answer to both sets of murders.'

'I still do not see what this has to do with me.'

Much to my dismay, he refilled his pipe from a filthy-looking old slipper and lit it, sending another gust of thick blue smoke into the room. 'I am now convinced that the person who wrote this scrawl was a man of the theatre, and that the key which will unlock its message is a deep knowledge of the works of Shakespeare — a deeper knowledge than even I myself possess, which is why I have called upon

35

you. As a former actress, you surely have more than a passing acquaintance with the Bard.'

I stared at him in wonderment. 'Well, yes, but what could possibly lead you to see a Shakespearean connection?'

'I will show you.' He pointed to the blackboard. 'As written, the message is meaningless, agreed?' Without waiting for my reply he rubbed out the last two words, *for nothing*, and asked, 'But what about this?' I had to admit that what was left made a complete, grammatically correct thought: *The Juwes are not the men who will be blamed*. Then I saw what he had obviously wanted me to see.

'It is written in iambic pentameter.'

'Precisely.'

'But can you really afford to discard the last two words?'

'Yes, because they are, literally and figuratively, *for nothing*,' he said. 'Now then, because of its spelling, the word *Juwes* stands out, so let us start with it. The most famous Jew in Shakespeare is, of course . . . ' He finished the sentence by writing out the word *Shylock* on the board. 'You see, I am not totally ignorant of the Swan of Avon. But note that the word is plural. Therefore I ask you, what other Shakespearean characters fall into that category?'

Goodness, how many years had it been since I had performed the classics with the Delancey Amateur Players? More than I cared to disclose. I tried to think back to our little group, conjuring up the faces of the other actors in the company and matching them with the roles they played. After a minute it came to me. 'There is another Jewish character in *The Merchant of Venice*, named Tubal,' I told him.

'Tubal,' Holmes repeated, jotting the word down on the board. Then his eyes lit up. 'I believe you have scored a hit on the first attempt!' After the word *Tubal* he wrote *cain*. 'Tubalcain' is the secret password of the Freemasons,' he said excitedly, 'which explains the Masonic spelling of the word *Jews*. Therefore, the answer to this devious equation would appear to be the word *cain*. Now, where does that lead us? The Biblical Cain, perhaps? The first murderer, slayer of his own brother?'

'Brother against brother,' I mused. 'Perhaps a reference to civil war?'

Holmes considered this. 'An interesting thought, and one that points towards an American, since wars in Europe are generally fought country against country, or religion against religion, but not brother against brother. Let us translate it back into our theme. Where do we find war, brotherly or otherwise, in the works of Shakespeare?'

'*Henry the Fifth* is set during the war between England and France.'

'You are invaluable, Watson.'

'*Mrs.* Watson, if you please. And my knowledge of the play comes from the fact that I understudied the role of Katherine once and had a terrible time with the language. It is partially written in French.'

He spun around and faced the blackboard. 'Partially written in French . . . of course! How could I have been so stupid?'

As I looked on, perplexed, he circled

the word *men* and then stepped back to look at the board. Just then our attention was drawn to a loud coughing coming from the door. Waving her way through the haze, and spluttering mightily, was Mrs. Hudson.

'Ooh, really, Mr. Holmes!' she cried. 'I have put up with your habits for a goodly number of years, but I'll be blamed if I will let this continue! My kitchen is full of smoke!'

'My abject apologies, Mrs. Hudson, but at the moment we are — ' Holmes stopped dead, and then a beaming smile broke out on his face. 'Mrs. Hudson, you are a jewel!' he cried. Then, throwing an arm around her shoulder, he began walking her back towards the door. 'I will make every effort to change my living habits, but for now I must ask you to go back to your kitchen, smoke-filled though it may be, while Mrs. Watson and I continue to work. And thank you so much.' With a gentle nudge he pushed her through the door and closed it behind her.

As I watched, puzzled, Holmes raced

back to the board, then circled *be blamed*. 'An English colloquialism, usually used in place of *be damned*, particularly by elderly landladies,' he said, a grin dancing over his lips. 'And this — ' He tapped the chalk on the circled word *men*. ' — translated into French, becomes *hommes*, which gives us . . . '

I watched, half in awe, half in disbelief, as he decoded the circled words and came up with: SHYLOCK HOMMES BE DAMNED. 'As I have long suspected, this scrawl was a personal taunt directed at me by the most fiendish killer London has ever known.'

In different circumstances I would have accredited Holmes's discovery of the message to coincidence, fuelled by megalomania. But in the potent, smoky atmosphere of his rooms, I was swayed. In addition, I could see yet another clue in the words that were left. 'Mr. Holmes, if you put the *t* from *not* after the *a* in *are*, and you get — '

'*Theatre*,' he finished, writing it on the board. 'And *will*, for Will Shakespeare, no doubt. This leaves us *o, n, w* and *h*. What do you make of that?'

My head was throbbing. 'Well, *w, h* and *o* spell *who*.'

'Which is the information we seek — *who*? The last remaining letter, *n*, is obviously the answer. It is most likely an initial.'

'Whose initial, Mr. Holmes?'

'I should say it is a person trained in the classical theatre, probably an actor, perhaps an American, though with knowledge of French and English colloquialisms; and a man with contempt for the police — for why else would he direct his message to me instead of the Yard? But to answer your question directly, Mrs. Watson, N is the initial of Jack the Ripper.'

* * *

'John, please answer honestly,' I said at supper the next evening. 'Has Mr. Holmes ever been so stunningly and brilliantly wrong that his conclusions, while impressive at first, later appear laughable?'

41

'Why do you ask?' John said glumly. He was still in his sulk.

'I keep thinking of the way he pulled words and meaning out of that scrawl. It rather reminded me of a fellow I once knew who was convinced that someone else had really written the works of Shakespeare and was forever twisting around the text and pulling out hidden clues that were not really there to support his theory.'

At this point Missy reappeared to clear our plates and bring John his evening *Times* (his reading at the table is a habit of which I fear I shall never be able to break him). Once she had gone, I continued: 'What if Mr. Holmes was guilty of the same thing? What if, after so many years of searching, he wanted to find a message so badly that . . . John, are you listening?'

My husband's face had gone pale as he stared at the newspaper. Finally he read: 'Early this morning police discovered the fourth victim of a killer being called the modern-day Jack the Ripper. The body of Mr. Francis Notting, a solicitor, was found behind his house in Stoke Newing-ton.'

Despite the warming fire in the hearth, I felt cold. *Notting* began with an N, the initial identified by Holmes as being the Ripper's. Yet this Notting had been one of the victims, not the killer.

Just then a thought struck me and I gasped, so loudly that John was startled. 'Amelia, are you all right?' he asked.

My voice quavered as I said, 'We must see Mr. Holmes immediately.'

'Whatever for?'

'I have just realized the meaning of the Ripper's scrawl.'

★   ★   ★

'You must think me a complete fool, Mrs. Watson,' Sherlock Holmes muttered as he studied the changes I had made to the scrawl.

'Nonsense,' I said, taking care not to further abrade his ego. 'I am sure you would have discovered it too, at some point.' Still, it was with some pride that I glanced back at the dusty blackboard, which had been erased and written more than a hundred times, and upon which was now printed:

THEDGEHUGHES ARNAUGHT THE MEN WHO WILL BE BLAMEFORT NOTTING.

'My congratulations, Mrs. Watson,' Holmes was saying, 'although someone has obviously beaten both of us to the solution.'

John, meanwhile, was muttering: '*Four men worked together to commit the Ripper killings; it is unbelievable.*'

'On the contrary, Watson,' Holmes said, 'it fits only too well. Consider the letters and postcards sent to the police and the newspapers from Jack the Ripper, each in a different handwriting; the conflicting descriptions of suspects from eyewitnesses; the reason Saucy Jack was so absurdly successful in eluding the entire Metropolitan police force. It all adds to a sum. One man took the chance of being caught only once, and if he subsequently became a suspect I daresay he would have had an unbreakable alibi for each of the other murders. It was a conspiracy as clever as it was diabolical, and one which is now about to play its final act.'

'Final act?'

'Think, Watson! There were *five* Ripper murders, not four; therefore one name remains inside the scrawl.'

John scanned the blackboard. 'I see no other names.'

'Watson, Watson,' Holmes cried, 'you see but you do not observe!' And in this instance I regretfully had to agree with him. Taking up the chalk, Holmes circled the words *will be*.

'Holmes, you can't mean — '

'Yes, Watson, the name of the fifth Ripper is *Wilby*, which can only mean Lord Wilby.'

'For heaven's sake, Holmes, the man is a member of government! Surely there are other men named Wilby.'

'None with enough power and influence to cover up such an unholy conspiracy for so long. If we could only get to him in time, we might be able to intercept the killer before he exacts his final revenge.'

'Revenge?'

'Yes, Watson, that is what this case is about: revenge. I was stupid not to realize it before.' Holmes was now in such a stage of nervous agitation that he appeared to emit smoke without the benefit of his pipe. 'But how can we get to Wilby when we don't even know where he lives?'

I suddenly remembered something I had spent a fortnight trying to block out. 'I have his address, Mr. Holmes!' I shouted, digging through my handbag until I found the calling card. 'He slipped it to me at Sir Melville's party. I told you the man was a beast, John.'

'There is not a moment to lose!' Holmes cried, snatching the card out of my hand and slipping it into his waistcoat pocket. Into his coat pocket he secreted a small revolver. 'Come along, Watson!'

'I am coming, too,' I said.

'Absolutely not!' John commanded.

'John, hear me out. By now Lord Wilby must know that he is to be the next victim. Do you think he is going to open his door to just anyone? As much as it disgusts me to contemplate, he *did* invite me to his home.'

'She is right, Watson,' Holmes said. 'Your wife may be our only way in. Now, come!'

John and Holmes flew down the flight of stairs to the street as though they had done it a thousand times before, which indeed they must have, while I struggled with my skirt every step of the way. Outside, Holmes was already hailing a cab. After offering the driver an extra half-crown if he could get us to Wilby's Mayfair address within ten minutes, we piled in for a coach ride the likes of which I had never experienced, and with luck never shall again.

We raced through the night like entrants in a steeplechase, bouncing over every cobble and brick in the streets, rounding every corner at such a speed that I felt we would surely tip over. To his credit the driver managed to keep the brougham upright while earning his bonus, though by the time we reached

Lord Wilby's home I felt like little pieces of my being had been shaken off and left behind.

Leaping from the coach, Holmes raced to Lord Wilby's door and began pounding on it. 'I fear we may be too late,' he said, thumping more and more violently. Finally he cried: 'Come, Watson, we must break it in!' and the two of them began throwing their combined weight against the door.

'John, be careful of your shoulder!' I called out, knowing he would be in agony the next morning. But he was on a case and nothing else mattered. When the bolt finally gave way Holmes and John rushed in to find a servant lying on the floor, a heavy bruise discolouring his forehead. With obvious effort the man then opened his eyes and whispered: 'Upstairs . . . the study.'

'Quickly!' Holmes shouted, pulling the revolver from his pocket and dashing up the wide staircase with John in pursuit. Lifting up my skirts almost above my knees, I dashed as well.

Voices were coming from behind one

of the upstairs panelled doors, which Holmes burst through, pistol in hand, closely followed by John. As I rushed in behind them, I could see Lord Wilby trapped in an overstuffed chair by a large brutish man dressed in a leather butcher's apron. One of the man's huge hands grasped Wilby's shoulder, holding him down, while the other held a knife to his throat.

'Do not make a move!' Holmes commanded.

'This no concern of yours!' the man growled back in a heavily accented voice.

'Murder is always a concern of mine, Vurczak.'

'Vurczak?' I blurted out. 'I thought he was dead.'

The man with the knife turned to look at me and I realized that, brutish or not, he was far too young to have been a suspect in the Ripper murders. Then the truth struck me. 'Vurczak the butcher was your father, wasn't he?'

The fierce scowl on his face faded away, revealing underneath the look of a lost little boy. 'I was six year old when they kill Papa,' he said. 'He was good man, and they kill him because this pig and his friends cut up those whores!' The knife scraped Wilby's neck. 'Tell them!' the man shouted.

'All right,' Wilby gasped. 'It's true. There were five of us who killed the prostitutes. Now let me go.'

But instead of letting him go, Vurczak pressed the knife even closer until a thin trickle of red ran down Lord Wilby's neck. At that instant the sound of a gunshot echoed through the room, startling everyone except Holmes. 'The next time I shall not miss,' he said. 'Now drop the knife!'

Throwing us a look of sheer hatred, the butcher lowered his arm and let the knife fall to the floor, then let Wilby loose.

'That's better,' Holmes said. 'Now, Lord Wilby, you may continue your confession.'

'Confession, Mr. Holmes? It *is* Holmes, is it not? Of course it is; who else would it be?' Wilby took out a handkerchief and pressed it to his neck. 'I have already been forced to admit a great deal, and I doubt telling you the rest can hurt me. After all, there is nothing you will be able to do about it. But before you rush to judgement, bear in mind how young we were then and how easy it was for young, affluent gentlemen to become bored. You see, there was nothing we could not afford, nothing we had not tried. Nothing except murder.'

I felt my blood chilling and reached out to John for warmth and support.

'We formed a little club, the five of us. The most exclusive club in London,' Wilby went on. 'We chose the East End to do our work for obvious reasons. It was already overpopulated by the expendables of society: the poor, the diseased, the criminal classes, immigrants. Of them all, prostitutes were the obvious victims.'

'Because they were women?' I demanded angrily.

'Because they were women who were used to being approached by strange men,' he sneered. 'Women who conducted their vile business in the shadows, unseen, the same way we needed to conduct our business. You know, when all is said and done, we were helping rid society of a scourge.'

'Even if that were true, it hardly explains the mutilation of the victims,' Holmes said.

'Oh, that. As part of the club initiation, proof was required that the deed had been done, and what could be more conclusive than a piece of the victim herself?' Had I been armed at that moment I might have tried to kill the man myself.

'But then something unexpected happened,' he continued. 'Jack the Ripper — my appellation, by the way — began to develop a life of his own. Before long the game had changed; it was no longer simply about the thrill of murder. Now it was about notoriety and danger and trying to outdo one another in brutality and audacity.

'We started writing to the police, taunting them, almost daring them to catch us. We even began leaving clues to our identities such as that message that Blamefort left on the wall, which he thought was so clever. That business of misspelling the word *Jews* was his revenge against the Freemasons, who had expelled him for some reason or other. He wanted them implicated, you see. At any rate, we knew the message would never be deciphered.'

'Yet it was,' Holmes said.

'But not by this lout,' Wilby said, gesturing contemptuously towards Vurczak. 'I doubt that he can even read. It was Thedgehughes who tipped the pot. He was always the weakest amongst us. I think it is fair to say that the knowledge of what he had done haunted him, and ultimately ruined him. In a drunken stupor one night it seems he blurted out the entire story to a stranger in a tavern, not realizing that he was confessing to his executioner.'

'He tell me everything,' Vurczak said. 'I kill him for it. Then I find the others and kill them too, these dogs that let my papa die for their sins!'

'Yes, yes, yes,' Wilby said impatiently. 'The ultimate irony, of course, is that our club was dissolved because of this oaf's sire. When he was killed by the mob I realized that we had far more to fear from the outraged public than the police. We decided to retire Jack, though I suspect a couple of the lads continued on their own over the years.'

Wilby reached into his coat for a cigar and with unbearable casualness, said: 'I trust no one minds if I smoke?'

'I would not object if you incinerated,' I replied.

Regarding me with annoyance, he muttered: 'What a mistake it was to give you my card. I should have realized immediately you were not the type.'

'Nor am I the type to attend murder trials,' I shot back, trying to control my voice, 'though I think I shall enjoy seeing you in the dock.'

'Oh, don't be stupid, madam,' he sneered, lighting his cigar. 'Nothing will happen to me. I am too important to His Majesty's Government. *There* is your killer, Holmes. Take him and get him out of here.'

'Take the gun, Watson,' Holmes said, 'and keep it pointed 🢚 straight at Vurczak's heart. If he makes a move of any kind, shoot him.'

Though obviously puzzled, John complied. Holmes went on: 'I caution you to remain still, Vurczak, for Dr. Watson is an excellent shot. As for you, Lord Wilby, I have no doubt that what you say is true. You would never be prosecuted for these crimes.'

'It is such a rare pleasure to deal with an intelligent man,' Wilby said. 'I will see Macnaghten in the morning about charges against this fellow. Now please leave, all of you.'

'As you wish,' Holmes said. 'You can put the gun away now, Watson; our business here is finished. We are leaving.' He turned and started towards the door.

The blasé veneer suddenly fell away from his lordship. 'What are you talking about?' he cried. 'You are taking this villain with you!'

'I think not,' said Holmes.

'But he is a murderer!'

'As are you, my lord, and all murderers must come to justice one way or other. The most desirable way is through the courts of this realm, though as you have so eloquently pointed out, that is not likely to happen. Therefore other methods must be considered.'

'Holmes, you cannot leave!' Lord Wilby cried. 'He will kill me!'

'If so, then I assure you I will do everything in my power to see that he is apprehended and brought to justice.'

'For God's sake, man, you cannot walk out of here and leave me defenceless!'

'Of course not,' Holmes replied, reaching into the pocket of his trousers and pulling out a jack-knife, which he opened and flung down on the floor. 'Defend yourself with that.'

As soon as we were out of the study Holmes slammed the door shut. From inside the room we heard the sounds of a struggle followed by a scream. Then the screaming stopped. 'What a pity we were too late,' Holmes said quietly.

* * *

For the next week the newspapers did little except decry the horrible tragedy and publish tribute after tribute to the late Lord Rodger Wilby. I could read none of them. Even though Wilby's servant and Holmes both offered the police a description of Vurczak the police were unable to find any trace of him.

'I doubt he will be seen again,' Mr. Holmes said as he peered out the window of his Baker Street den, into which Mrs. Hudson was bringing a pot of piping hot tea and a tray of cakes. 'He is most likely on board a ship headed for parts unknown by now.'

'Will the truth ever be made public?' I asked.

'Perhaps someday,' he said, then reached for his top hat and walking stick. 'I must leave you now.'

'Where on earth are you off to?' John asked, helping himself to a tea cake.

'I have an appointment with Sir Melville Macnaghten,' Holmes said, flashing one of those electric, quicksilver smiles. 'I am sure Mrs. Hudson will permit you to stay as long as you like. Goodbye.' He then dashed out of the rooms like the White Rabbit.

As John happily chatted with his former

landlady, I scanned the cluttered rooms he used to call home. Invariably my gaze returned to the blackboard, on which the horrid scrawl was still printed. As I concentrated on it I realized that one more name had to be added to make it complete and provide the final, ironic message. Walking over to the board I erased the words, then picked up the chalk and began to write.

'What on earth are you doing?' John asked, but I did not answer. I simply stepped back, allowing him to read:

THEDGEHUGHES, ARNAUGHT, WILBY, BLAMEFORT, NOTTING: THE MEN WHO VURCZAK.

The Adventure of the
Damsel in Grey

'A holiday!' I cried. 'John, do you really mean it?'

'Absolutely,' my husband answered. 'I have already made all the arrangements and cleared my appointment calendar for the next week.'

'Darling, what brought this on?'

'I simply came to the conclusion that I have not been giving you the attention you deserve, what between my practice and, well, you know . . . '

I smiled, knowing indeed.

'And since we never had a honeymoon as such, I thought that this might make up for it.'

'Oh, John,' I sighed, running into his arms, not caring that I must have resembled the twittering witless heroine from a third-rate melodrama. 'Where are we going? No, wait, don't tell me. France? Spain?'

'My dear, we are on our way to Nether — '

'The Netherlands! How delightful!'

John cleared his throat self-consciously. 'Actually, Amelia, we are going to Nether Sworthing.'

'We are going *where*, dear?'

'Nether Sworthing. It is a delightful little village in the Cotswolds, a mere two-hour journey by train.'

I stepped back from his embrace, trying to mask my disappointment with a frozen smile. 'And where did you hear about this Swollen Nothing?'

'*Nether Sworthing*,' John corrected, though I had heard him perfectly well the first time. Sarcasm, alas, is frequently lost on my husband. 'I was there a number of years ago, with Holmes, working on a case.'

'I should have guessed,' I said. While there are many privileges in being the wife of Dr. John H. Watson, albeit the second to hold the title, the ever-present umbra of Mr. Sherlock Holmes, which looms over us like the overpowering memory of a cherished first wife, is not one of them. It is not that I dislike Mr. Holmes, exactly. In my few, undeniably eventful experiences with him, he has struck me as being entirely too vulnerable to truly dislike, despite that carefully formed veneer of cold rationality. On one or two occasions he has even shown me great kindness, which, I understand, is quite singular (to use John's favourite word) in his history of dealings with the opposite sex. But those few instances are weighed against the many evenings I have spent alone and desperately lonely, waiting for my husband to return from his latest Holmesian escapade, vainly wishing that the 'world's greatest detective' would retire and let us conduct our own lives in peace.

My sudden change of mood at the mention of Holmes's name should have been palpable to anyone, though John remained oblivious, continuing to prattle on about this particular Cotswold Eden.

'The next thing I know, I get a letter from this fellow Reeves, whom Holmes and I met there years ago, stating that he has taken over the village inn and inviting me down to stay with him. And I thought: 'What a superb idea!' The village is peaceful, quiet and charming, the perfect place to leave the problems of the great city behind and just relax. You will love it, Amelia, I promise.'

Honestly, how could I continue to be cross with him when he was trying so valiantly to please me? 'I will do my best to adore the place, darling,' I said, and meant it.

Three days later we boarded the train at Paddington, and after a refreshingly uneventful journey stepped off at the station in Moreton-at-Marsh, which was as close as we could get by rail to Nether Sworthing. No sooner had John wrestled our bags to the platform than a voice called: 'Ho! Dr. Watson! Over here!'

'Reeves!' John called back, hailing a tall, powerful-looking man who was dressed for the country in tweeds and a deerstalker cap (heaven help us!), the latter evenly perched atop his woolly head. Gabriel Reeves sprinted to us, grabbed John's hand and shook it vigorously. 'What a pleasure to see you again, Doctor!' he bellowed. Having pumped John's hand dry, he turned to me and grinned broadly. 'And you must be Mrs. Watson. Your servant, madam,' he said, taking my gloved hand and kissing in an awkward fashion that indicated he was not very experienced in such greetings.

Largely through Mr. Reeves's efforts, our bags were hauled across the platform and loaded onto a stately landau, which was being driven by a boy who looked barely old enough to handle the reins, but proved to be quite capable once we were underway. Within minutes we were enjoying the warm, inviting green of the countryside.

Whatever the peculiarities of its name, Nether Sworthing was a beautiful little village, abounding in scenery that would have inspired a landscape painter from the Royal Academy. An arching stone bridge spanned a gently flowing stream, which in turn coursed past rows of compact stone cottages. In the centre of the village sat an ancient market cross, and resting atop a nearby green rise was an equally ancient church.

Leaning towards us, Mr. Reeves said: 'Norman.'

'No, John,' replied my husband, 'though I rarely stand on formality. Just plain Watson will do.'

'I believe he means the church, darling,' I said.

'That's right,' Reeves acknowledged. 'It was built in 1163, and is as fine an example of Norman architecture as you will find anywhere in England. Ah, here we are.'

The carriage stopped in front of a two-story stone building identified as the Commonwealth Inn. As John helped me down, Mr. Reeves and the driver began to take our bags inside.

The public house of the inn was surprisingly dark and musty-smelling, a dreary atmosphere that was brightened only by the sunny demeanour of a plump, cheerful woman whom our host introduced as his 'lady wife', Emily. We proceeded upstairs to our room which, although small, was certainly comfortable and offered a pleasing view of the village. After the youthful driver had brought up the last of our bags, John withdrew a sixpence from his pocket and handed it to him.

'Thank you, Dr. Watson, sir,' the lad responded.

John studied him. 'How did you know my name?'

'Oh, I remember you right well, sir, you and Mr. Holmes. Why, he paid me a shilling for each message I carried for him when you and he was here before.'

'Good heavens, you must be young Daniel!' John said, delighted at the discovery. 'I never would have recognized you. What a strapping young fellow you've become!'

Daniel beamed. 'Thank you, sir. If there's anything else you'll be requiring while you're here, you just let me know.' In an awkwardly earnest parody of a military about-face, the young man spun on his heel and strode away.

'Well, it appears that Mr. Holmes has urchins at his disposal in every corner of the realm.'

'I can hardly believe it is the same lad! I must write to Holmes immediately and tell him.'

'You will do no such thing. We are here

to enjoy ourselves, *by* ourselves. There will be plenty to tell Mr. Holmes after we've returned to London.' If only I had realized then how prophetic that statement would be!

After unpacking and settling in, we returned to the public house, which was now open and already populated by a handful of customers. As soon as he saw John, Mr. Reeves pumped a glass of dark, cloudy bitter and held it out. 'Here, Dr. Watson, try this,' he said. 'I'm trying my hand at brewing my own, and I'd be interested in your opinion.'

John took a sip and his expression told all, though he managed to remain polite. 'It's ... uh ... it's very interesting, though perhaps a bit strong.'

'It makes a decent shandy, though,' Mrs. Reeves said, wiping her plump hands on her apron as she joined her husband behind the bar. 'Can I get you one, luv?'

'Oh, no, thank you,' I replied. Shandy, in my opinion, was loathsome enough when it was made with good beer.

After a few more patrons had entered

the pub our host shattered the calm by loudly introducing John as *the* Dr. John Watson of London, friend and chronicler of the great and wondrous Mr. Sherlock Holmes! Suddenly John was the centre of attention, though if he felt uncomfortable in that position he certainly did not show it.

If nothing else, my years as an ingénue on the amateur stage had taught me when to make an exit, and as I did not particularly wish to spend the rest of the day listening to the baldly romanticized adventures of Mr. Sherlock Holmes, I decided to take advantage of my *exeunt* cue.

'Mrs. Reeves,' I called, motioning her to me, 'would you be so good as to tell me what there is to see in your village?'

'See? In Nether Sworthing?' She laughed. 'The church is about the only thing worth seeing, luv. It should be open now, though if it isn't, just knock up the sexton and he'll let you in.'

'Thank you. And could you please let my husband know that I went out for a bit? He appears to be a tad preoccupied at the moment.' With that, I slipped outside.

Finding the church posed no problem, since it was visible from every part of the village. Just as Mrs. Reeves had predicted, the doors were indeed open. As I crept inside, a chill came over me: not a dankness like the one I had left behind in the pub, but a stony, tomblike cold. Still, the little church was serenely beautiful, with ornately carved pews and faded frescoes, apparently Norman in origin, adorning the walls. My footsteps echoed back as I walked towards the chancel, seating myself in the front pew. I spent several minutes in reverent silence, enveloped in a stillness so complete that when the sighing voice suddenly came from somewhere behind me, it echoed through the walls like the howling wind.

I turned around a saw a young woman standing at the rear of the church. Her long, dark hair seemed to stand away from her face as though it were windblown. She was dressed completely in grey, and her clothing seemed of a very old fashion. Even from that distance I could read the expression of fear on her face.

'Help me,' she said.

'What is wrong?' I called back.

'My father wants to kill me!'

'What?'

She looked sharply to the side, as though alerted by a sound that I was unable to hear, and with a sudden gasp bolted from the spot.

'Wait!' I cried, springing out of the pew and running up the aisle. I would swear under oath that at no time had I taken my gaze away from the spot where the woman had stood; yet when I got there, there was no sign of another human being. The woman had simply vanished.

'This cannot be,' I muttered, surveying the interior of the church once more. The woman was nowhere to be found.

Leaving the church, I practically ran back to the public house, trying to shake off the cold, uneasy feeling that had overtaken me. Upon returning, I found that John was still enjoying his position centre stage and was relating one of his more recently published stories, a wild tale of a mad dog running loose on the moors.

My distress must have shown as I made my way to the bar, since our host asked: 'Mrs. Watson, are you all right?'

'I've had the most extraordinary experience,' I said. 'I was sitting in the church — alone, I thought — and this young woman came in, dressed completely in grey, and she asked for my help.'

'You've seen her, then?' Mr. Reeves interjected, loudly and urgently enough to silence my husband, who asked: 'Is something wrong?'

'I don't know,' I said. 'There was a young woman in the church who seemed distressed and frightened, and she said that her father wanted to kill her.'

A low chorus of murmuring went through the pub, and I quickly realized that all eyes had turned away from John and were now focused on me.

'She obviously needs help,' I went on. 'We must find her.'

'I'm afraid you're too late,' Mr. Reeves said matter-of-factly. 'Her father was the squire of Nether Sworthing, and in a drunken rage over her elopement to a commoner, he did kill her. More than a hundred and fifty years ago.'

'I'm afraid I don't understand.'

'You have seen the Damsel in Grey, Mrs. Watson. Our local ghost.'

Suddenly exhausted, and more than a little confused, I quickly retired to our room. But by that evening the story of my encounter with the 'ghost' had spread over the village like a flooding river, and even our attempt to take our dinner was so interrupted by locals asking for details of my 'sighting' that Mr. Reeves finally had to intervene.

The situation was even worse on the following day when our every movement was tracked by a small army of local cottagers, all hoping to be present should the phantom make a return appearance. My repeated attempts to explain that I did not even believe in the existence of ghosts fell on deaf ears, and hopes of enjoying a relaxing holiday in the country had vanished as completely as the Damsel herself.

As we prepared for bed at the end of our second day as visiting curiosities, John glumly suggested: 'Why don't we tell everyone that it was a mistake; that you really saw nothing at all?'

'I fear it has spread too far, John; no one in the village would believe that now. Besides, it was *not* a mistake. I *did* see that girl.'

'What a singular problem,' John sighed. 'I wonder what Holmes would make of it?'

'And you will continue to wonder, darling, in complete silence, if you have any hopes of turning this into a honeymoon,' I replied, climbing into the large, downy bed.

We slept comfortably. Early the next morning, however, we were awakened by a commotion outside our room, punctuated by someone pounding on our door and crying, 'Dr. Watson! Dr. Watson!'

'What on earth . . . ?' John muttered, climbing out of bed and skipping over the cold floor while trying to get his arms in his dressing gown. Opening the door, he found Daniel.

'Come quick, sir, there's been an accident!'

'Let me get dressed. I'll be right down.' We both dressed in record time, though the improperly aligned buttons of John's shirt advertised his haste. Daniel rushed us outside, where a horrible sight was waiting for us. The body of a young woman lay crumpled in a small garden at the side of the inn.

Upon seeing her face, I gasped. 'It is she!' I shouted. 'That is the woman I saw in the church!'

'Great Scott!' John cried. 'Are you sure?'

Bracing myself, I knelt down to examine her more closely. A modern shirtwaist and skirt had replaced the archaic grey dress, and most of her left temple was discoloured by a dark, ugly bruise. But even so, there was no mistaking her. 'I am positive,' I said. 'This is the Damsel in Grey.'

'Well, this woman certainly did not die a hundred and fifty years ago,' John replied. 'She has been dead for maybe six or seven hours.'

I had started to rise again when I detected a peculiar odour — peculiar, at least, for the circumstances. I leaned down until my nose was just above her blouse.

'Amelia, what on earth are you doing?' John asked.

'Lemon. I detect the scent of lemon on her clothes.'

'What can that possibly mean?'

'I am sure I don't know, but — '

My thoughts were interrupted by the sudden reappearance of Daniel, who notified John that the constable from the neighbouring village had been sent for. 'So, sir,' he added, 'have you figured out how she was killed?'

'Blow to the head, I should think.'

'Hmmm, or maybe a fall from a height,' Daniel said, directing our attention to an open upstairs window above where the body lay. 'She might have fallen from that window and hit her head on one of these rocks.'

'Yes, Daniel, I daresay you could be right,' John said, clearly impressed by the deduction. 'Now, if you could only tell us who she is.'

'Her name is Sarah Wells,' said another voice; and I looked up to see the ashen, stunned face of our host, Mr. Reeves. 'Come inside, please, and I will tell you everything.'

'Daniel, see if you can find a blanket to cover her with until the police arrive,' John said, and the lad sprinted away.

I remained where I was, having discovered another puzzling element. 'I'll be there in a second, dear,' I called to John. 'I want to catch my breath first.'

Within seconds Daniel had returned with the blanket, which smelled like a stable. 'Best I could do on quick notice,' he confessed.

'Daniel, what do you make of these?' I asked, fingering two depressions in the ground.

'Looks like footprints, only deeper.'

'My thoughts exactly. Would you mind terribly holding up her leg?' He did as I asked, with no outward sign of discomfort, which was more than I could say for myself as I gingerly slipped off one of the dead woman's shoes. It fit perfectly into one of the depressions. 'This matter gets more puzzling by the second,' I noted.

'How so, ma'am?'

'Because of the depth of the prints. The ground is not wet or spongy enough for her feet to have sunk down into it. She would have had to hit the ground with great force to make these marks.'

'Right, like if she fell out of a window.'

'But only if she fell *feet first*. Yet the wound on her temple implies she landed head first. How can a person do both at the same time? Unless . . . '

'Unless?'

The only possible explanation was not a very pleasant one to contemplate. 'I will have to explain later,' I said. 'Now I must rejoin my husband — and for the time being, Daniel, let us not tell anyone else about these footprints.'

'If you say so, ma'am.'

I left him to cover the body of poor Sarah and stepped to the door of the public house, which was quickly opened by Mrs. Reeves. Once I was inside, she equally quickly closed and locked it again. Her husband was slumped down in a chair, still ashen.

'I honestly saw no harm in the deception,' he said.

'What have I missed?' I asked.

I could tell from John's manner that something in our host's statement thus far had already irritated him. 'It seems,' he began, 'that we have been the victims of an insidious prank. That poor girl now lying dead was an actress from London, hired by Reeves to impersonate the ghost specifically for our benefit.'

'Oh, good heavens,' I cried. 'But why our benefit?'

Never taking his gaze from the floor, Mr. Reeves said meekly: 'I thought we might be able to fire up Dr. Watson's imagination enough that he would write a Sherlock Holmes story centred around our local legend, like he did with the hound of Dartmoor.'

'My imagination!' John roared. 'My dear Reeves, the stories I write concerning the exploits of my friend, Mr. Sherlock Holmes, are based on actual facts and are not the products of my imagination!'

'Gently, darling, gently,' I said, trying to

calm him down. Then turning to the innkeeper, I asked: 'But even if he were to write such a tale, how would that benefit you?'

'By drawing tourists into the village. Interest in spiritualism is growing. Once the reading public learned of an actual, documented ghostly sighting, presented by a reputable author, people would flock to Nether Sworthing, hoping for the chance to see the Damsel themselves. And they would, by necessity, take lodging here at the inn.'

'And that was why you invited us up here,' John said bitterly. 'You were merely using us as part of this bizarre plan.'

'Dr. Watson, every farthing I own has been sunk into this lodging house, and the return has not been forthcoming,' Reeves declared. 'I had to do something. And it would have worked, if only poor Sarah hadn't panicked.'

'I do not follow you,' John said.

The innkeeper sighed deeply. 'Of all the actresses I interviewed, Sarah was the most desperate for work. She said she would do anything for a job and agreed to come here without fully realizing what would be required of her. You see, in order for her appearances as the Damsel to be effective, she had to remain hidden at all other times. We lodged her upstairs and forbade her to leave her room, under penalty of forfeiting her pay. Meals and other necessities were brought up to her. At first, she occupied her time studying the legend of the Damsel and perfecting her performance, but then she became restless. Even one day can seem like an eternity when it is spent shut in and alone.'

Reeves finally faced us directly, all life seeming to have drained from his eyes. 'After a while she became careless,' he went on. 'She began to slip out in the evenings when she thought we were asleep. I caught her one night near the church. Fortunately, nobody else had seen her, but I could no longer afford to take chances. After that, we started locking her in her room.'

'Good Lord,' John muttered.

'There was no alternative, Doctor. We thought it would prevent any further attempts at escape until her role, as it were, had been completed. Her time finally came when your wife said she wanted to see the church. As soon as you had gone, Mrs. Watson, Emily went upstairs and told Sarah to get ready; and while you were holding the attention of the customers, Doctor, Em slipped Sarah out the back door and took her to the church.

'After her appearance as the Damsel, she hid in the church and remained there until after dark, when I was able to go get her. By then, though, she'd managed to get herself all worked up. She demanded her money, saying she'd had enough of the village, the Damsel and the whole plan, and wanted to leave as soon as possible. There was nothing I could do but agree. I told her I would pay her off as soon as we were back at the inn. But once I had got her here . . . ' His voice began to falter.

'You locked her back inside her room,' John said.

The innkeeper nodded, saying: 'I wanted one more appearance before I let her go. It didn't even dawn on me that she might try to get out through the window.'

'So you think she fell to her death during an escape attempt?'

'That is what I believe. May God have mercy on her soul, and mine also.'

The sound of the door opening prevented me from giving the wretched man a very large piece of my mind regarding his irresponsible and callous behaviour towards a poor unfortunate girl. A stout, smug-looking police constable sauntered into the public house, quickly followed by Daniel, who announced: 'This is Constable Trout.'

'I'll take it from here, son, if you don't mind,' the policeman said, puffing up his chest. 'Now then, let's just start from the beginning, if you please.'

As the story was tumbling out once more, I slipped unobtrusively to Daniel's side and in a hushed voice said: 'I distinctly noticed that Mrs. Reeves locked the door after I came in. How did you get in just now?'

'Mr. Reeves gave me a master key when

I started working for him,' he answered.

It took a fair amount of wheedling, but I finally managed to persuade Daniel to let me borrow the key. Constable Trout — who, save for his heavy-lidded eyes, rather resembled one — was now harrumphing mightily and looking in my direction.

'If *I* may be permitted to speak now, madam?' he blustered. 'This looks to me like an open-and-shut case of accidental death, though I assure you I shall be fully apprising my superiors of the doubtable actions that resulted in this tragedy.' He stopped to glare recriminatingly at Mr. and Mrs. Reeves before adding: 'And they may have more to say about this.'

Rushing to my husband's side, I clapped a hand to my forehead and moaned: 'I suddenly feel so faint. Help me upstairs, darling.'

'We will be in our room should anyone require us further,' John announced, then walked me to the stairs. Once we had reached the landing, he whispered: 'I hope the stage performances of your youth were more accomplished than that one, my dear. What are you up to?'

Ignoring his criticism (I felt I had been quite convincing), I proceeded down the hallway, past our own room, and stopped in front of another door, which was locked. 'Yes, this must be it.'

'Amelia, what the devil are you doing?'

'I want to see the girl's room,' I said, producing the master key.

'Where did you get that?' John demanded, but before he could finish his protest I was inside the room. Although the furnishings were identical to those in our room, it was strewn with loose articles of clothing and other clutter, and quite dirty.

'What are you looking for?' John asked.

In truth I did not know myself, until I found it. 'Look at this,' I said, crouching down next to a circular spot on the stone hearth, which had recently been washed. It was, in fact, the only clean spot in the entire room.

'Why would someone wash a hearth-stone but leave the rest of the place so filthy?' John asked.

I managed to subdue an overpowering

urge to say 'Elementary,' answering instead: 'To wash off traces of blood, I would imagine.'

John's eyes grew wide. 'Amelia, do you mean to tell me that — '

'I am convinced Sarah died in this room and was pushed out of the window to make it look like an accident or a suicide. The real question is, who would want to kill her?'

'We had better advise the constable of this before he leaves,' John said.

'That pompous baboon? You saw the manner in which he spoke to me. I hardly think he would take my advice about anything. No, darling, I must think this one out for myself. Let us go back to our room.'

We left the dead girl's room as surreptitiously as we had entered it, and returned to our own suite. 'I must clear my head,' I said. 'Please hand me that book.' As I began perusing *Barnaby Rudge* by Mr. Dickens, an author whose shining brilliance has always provoked a heightened clarity in my own mind, John decided to lie down.

In between paragraphs I set about thinking over the facts of the tragedy. As I recounted the individual pieces of this bizarre puzzle, many began to fit together. Only one fit nowhere: the puzzling smell of lemon on the dead girl's clothing.

'Oh, this is maddening,' I muttered, snapping the book shut.

'Are you all right, dear?' came John's voice.

'I'm sorry, darling. I thought you were asleep.'

He rolled over on the bed to face me. 'How can I sleep when I am tortured by the inescapable conclusion that my friend Reeves is a murderer?'

'Mr. Reeves, John? Do you really think so?'

'Look at the facts, Amelia. A woman is killed inside a room that is always kept locked. That means the killer must have possessed a key. Who other than Reeves would have had a key?'

'Well, Daniel, for one, but why would Daniel . . . *Oh!*' I cried, putting a hand to my head.

'I know that gesture,' John said,

suddenly sitting up, and it pleased me to detect in him some small trace of the excitement he normally reserved for his exploits with the great Mr. Holmes. 'You have figured it all out, haven't you?'

'Yes, darling. I believe I know who killed Sarah, though I pray I am wrong. Come along; I suddenly feel like a drink.'

'At this hour?' John protested, but I had already started for the stairs, leaving him no choice but to follow.

Constable Trout had departed, leaving the sombre tableau of our host and hostess and Daniel grimly going about their chores in preparation to open the public house. 'I hope we never have to go through that again,' the innkeeper said bitterly as he wiped dry a glass. 'That blighter nearly upset my Em to tears.'

'He was rather a brute,' I concurred. Then, turning to Emily Reeves, I said: 'I know the bar is not officially open yet, but there has been so much excitement already this morning, I wonder if I could prevail upon you to make a shandy for me. It may help calm my nerves.'

'Coming right up, luv,' she said,

seemingly happy to oblige. 'I often take a bit o' the stuff myself when I get worked into a frazzle.'

I watched carefully as she pumped a glass half-full of her husband's noxious bitter. Then from a place underneath the bar she carefully selected three lemons, which she sliced open and squeezed into a separate glass, adding in water and a touch of sugar. She poured this concoction into the beer and set it down in front of me, then wiped her hands on her apron.

'Thank you,' I said, forcing myself to take a sip. It was abominable, though I managed to keep a smile on my face (and John dares to question my acting ability!). 'This must be just like the one you made right before you dropped Sarah's body out of the window.'

'Oh, aye, that was — ' Mrs. Reeves stopped suddenly, her face turning pale.

'What are you saying, Mrs. Watson?' her husband demanded.

'Something that gives me no pleasure, I assure you. But you were the one who caused her death, were you not, Mrs. Reeves?'

'It wasn't my fault — not entirely,' she cried. 'The poor lamb; being cooped up in that room had driven her half-mad. Getting locked back up after she'd been let out must have been the last straw. She was waiting for me when I took her dinner up that night. She jumped on me, demanding the key. She didn't even want the money, she said; she just wanted to be let out. She tried to choke me.' The woman pulled down the high collar of her dress to reveal rows of swollen red scratches.

'Good heavens, those need to be treated,' John said, dashing upstairs for the small medical bag he is never without.

'Go on, Mrs. Reeves,' I said.

'Well, I fought back any way that I could. I managed to get my hands under her and I shoved as hard as I could. She went back, all right — back over a table and down, and then I heard this horrible sound. She'd hit her head on the hearth.'

John had now returned and was pulling a jar of salve from his bag to dab onto the scratches.

'I knew she was dead,' Mrs. Reeves

continued tearfully, 'but there were people downstairs. So I locked the door and left her there. Later, after closing, I made myself a shandy for courage and went back up. I thought that maybe I could make it look like an accident after all. I wrapped my apron around her, so's I didn't have to touch her, and dragged her over to the window. It took some doing, but I got her through. Then I cleaned up the spot where she'd hit her head and just waited for her to be found in the morning.' She dabbed her eyes with the corner of her apron. 'How did you know it was me, luv?'

'The smell of lemon was on her clothes,' I replied, 'something I could not explain until I remembered you offering me a shandy, which is made with lemonade. Your apron that night must have been still damp with lemon juice when you wrapped it around her.'

'So am I to go to prison because of a shandy?' she asked helplessly.

'There is no question that we will have to inform the authorities,' John said, 'though I think these scratches will present a good case for self-defence. You may count on me to testify on your behalf when the time comes.' Dear, considerate John.

As Gabriel Reeves stoically comforted his sobbing wife, Daniel was dispatched once more to intercept the constable and bring him back. There was nothing else for John and me to do but return to our room and begin packing. How differently this holiday had turned out from our original intent!

'I cannot believe all this happened simply because Reeves wanted me to write a ghost story,' John said, neatly folding one of his shirts and placing it in the suitcase.

'Never underestimate the power of fiction, darling.'

'And that's another thing — it still rankles me that he seems to think I make these stories up! I am simply relating my experiences with Holmes.'

'Come, now, even you must admit that you have on occasion exaggerated matters.'

'Not a bit!'

'Oh, really, John — a disgruntled tenant farmer turns a dog loose on the landowner, and you play it up as the Hound of Hell.'

'It *was* a Hound of Hell! At least, that is what it looked like in the dark.'

I was unable to stifle a giggle, which quickly turned into a spasm of laughter, which further infuriated John, sending him into a prolonged silence.

After a time, though, and with a decidedly wicked glint in his eye, he said: 'You know, Amelia, perhaps I should write up this little adventure. It was, after all, a singular piece of deduction, and I don't suppose you would really mind if I changed things around to make it Holmes who solved the case, would you?'

'You do that, darling,' I purred, giving him a wicked look of my own, 'and you might just find yourself relocating back to Baker Street.'

The Adventure of the Glass House

'Harry!' I cried, 'Harry Benbow! Heavens, is it really you?'

The small figure in the cloth cap turned and regarded me for a moment, then his face lit up like a brazier. 'Amelia Pettigrew!' he shouted, then practically danced his way through the half-dozen Covent Garden flower carts that separated us.

'Little Amelia Pettigrew,' he repeated. 'Gor, I can't believe it!' At first I thought he was going to take me in a mad embrace, which would have all but crushed the bouquet of red roses I was holding; but he settled for clasping my free hand in both of his. 'How long has it been?'

'Too long, Harry,' I said, 'and it is Amelia Watson now.'

'No kidding! Our little Amelia found herself a feller, did she? I hope he's not an actor.'

'No, Harry, he's a doctor, whose chief fault is polluting the air of our home with his pipe, which is why I am out buying flowers. But tell me, what you are up to?'

'Oh, 'bout five foot,' he said, as I knew he would; and I laughed, as he knew I would. It was easily twenty years since I had last seen Harry Benbow, at which time we were both in the same amateur theatrical troupe, I being the young (very young, mind you) ingénue, while Harry was the lead comedian. But the years had not dimmed his energy, nor his ability to make me laugh.

'I've been doing a bit o' this and that,' he went on. 'But listen, I'm acting again.'

'How wonderful! What theatre?'

'Well, it's not for the theatre, it's for the filums. You know, moving pictures? Surely you've heard about 'em.'

In truth, I knew very little about moving images projected onto a screen. I had heard just enough about them to know that some people considered them a vulgar novelty, while others felt they were the future of entertainment. Harry was obviously among the latter.

'This bloke from America — Nick Johnson, his name is — he's doing some picture work over here, so who's the first person he calls? Harry Benbow.' His pride was about to burst through his well-worn waistcoat. Then he did a 'take' and slapped himself on the forehead with his palm. 'Gor, it's Providence what brought us together today! We need an actress, and 'ere you are! Amelia, how would you like to be in pictures?'

'Me?'

'Sure! We had a girl drop out yesterday and there's a part open now. You'd be perfect for it.'

'But Harry, I can't go back to acting. I'm a respectable married woman now.'

'Oh, if that's what's bothering you, wait 'til you meet our leading lady. Just come round and meet Mr. Johnson; and if you still say no, then no 'arm done. The stage is only a quick step up the road from here.'

A quick step indeed! My feet were aching by the time we reached a glass hothouse, the kind used for growing plants, at the far end of Coram's Field.

Even before we had entered the structure, I could hear the sounds of pandemonium inside.

People scurried back and forth in the building, brightly illuminated by the sunlight beaming in through the ridged glass roof. All four walls, though, had been covered with black drapes. At one end of the glass house was a makeshift stage with three wall flats, painted and decorated as a chamber of a grand palace. Standing on this set was a woman dressed, jewelled and bewigged in such a way that could only signify a queen, while hovering around her were three men in soldier uniforms of the Commonwealth era.

'Don't tell me, Harry; let me guess. *The Three Musketeers?*'

'Presented for the first time ever on filum,' he said brightly, 'and with a sterling cast, including yours truly as Planchet.'

'But why are you doing this in a hothouse?'

'The very same question I asked when summoned to become a member of this company, and one that Mr. Johnson put straight. See, the camera needs a lot of light or else nothing shows up on the filum, and the best source of that light is the good ol' sun. Some of the lesser filum companies, I hear tell, builds their sets in the open and then spends the whole day fighting the wind. But our Mr. Johnson, he's a clever one. He sets up inside a glass 'ouse, which allows you to let the light in but keeps the breeze out. Come on, ducks, let me introduce you to him.'

Harry led me through the chaos to a man in shirtsleeves who appeared to be the calm in the centre of the storm. He was tall — taller even than Mr. Holmes — and was forced to bend nearly in half in order to peer through the eyepiece of a crank-driven contraption that was attached to a three-legged stand, which I presumed to be the moving-picture camera.

'Mr. Johnson!' Harry called out, bouncing up and down like a ball to gain his attention.

'Oh, there you are Harry,' the man said in an accent that sounded Irish by way of Canada. Then I remembered Harry telling me the man was an American. 'Did you bring the flowers?' he asked.

'Oh, Gor, I forgot!' Harry moaned.

'You may borrow my roses if you need them urgently,' I jumped in.

The tall man directed his gaze upon me. 'And you are . . . ?'

'Mr. Johnson, I have solved our casting problem,' Harry announced. 'This is Amelia Pettigrew, who would be perfect as Constance.'

The producer sized me up toe to head. 'Have you ever acted before, Miss Pettigrew?' he asked; but before I could answer, Harry chimed in with, 'She and I trod the boards together with the Delancey Players,' pointedly leaving out the word *amateur*.

'Fine, be here tomorrow morning at nine o'clock sharp,' Mr. Johnson said. 'And thank you for the flowers.' He strode over to a table on the set and placed them in a vase.

'Our Mr. Johnson's a tartar for authenticity,' Harry said admiringly. 'No artificial flowers for his filum!'

'But I only offered to *lend* him my

roses,' I said plaintively.

'Oh, Amelia, what's a few roses compared to the beginning of a whole new career? Just think of it: Benbow and Pettigrew together again. Look, I've got to go get into costume now, but I will see you tomorrow.' Then, like a rubber ball, he bounced into the middle of the chaos and disappeared.

I have to admit that, while my mind was reeling at the pace with which everything had transpired, I found the prospect of performing again rather exciting. How John would have felt about it was another matter, but one into which I could not enquire, since he was away visiting an ailing member of his old army regiment. I journeyed home (on the omnibus this time) to prepare for my debut on the morrow as a 'filum' actress!

Arriving at the appointed time the next day, I found the activity in the glass house even more chaotic. I was immediately taken in hand by Harry, who was wearing an ill-fitting servant's costume. In short order he introduced me to four young men in Musketeer uniforms who appeared more concerned with their dice game than with the production, and a gentleman named Maurice Denby who was enacting the role of Louis the Thirteenth. Finally, we came to the woman I had seen the day before in a queen's raiment.

'This, Amelia, is our star,' Harry said respectfully. 'May I present Lady Ashford, wife of the Right Honourable Earl of Ashford.'

'Of the Ashford Diamonds?' I gasped.

'The same,' she replied pleasantly. 'And I can read on your face the question nearly everyone else has asked: what am I doing in these surroundings?'

I confessed that the question had occurred to me.

'I will tell you, then. A week or so back Mr. Johnson contacted us, enquiring as to whether he could photograph my husband's ancestral home, Notley Court, as a background for his film. Unfortunately, George was rather against it; but then when the young man asked if he could photograph me instead as the Queen of France, it was simply too flattering to refuse. You see,' she said conspiratorially, 'I have long harboured a secret desire to perform.'

I had the pleasure of chatting with her for a few more minutes before she and Harry were called away by a sullen, plain-looking young woman who examined and adjusted their costumes.

Suddenly left to fend for myself, I did my best to stay out of the way of the people who were dashing back and forth, ultimately deciding that the safest place to stand was next to the moving-picture camera itself. The contraption looked like a tiny steamer trunk with a lens in the front and a crank on the side. Unable to stifle my curiosity, I tested the crank and heard a whirring sound coming from inside the box.

Then I heard a voice shouting: 'Don't touch that!'

Letting go of the crank, I turned to see Nick Johnson running towards me. 'Please, Miss Pettigrew, never touch the camera. If you were to accidentally open the magazine you would expose the film to light and ruin the image, and I would hate to lose all of the footage we shot yesterday.'

'Oh, I am sorry,' I stammered.

'You should be getting into costume, anyway. Beryl!' he called, and the plain young woman reappeared out of the hurly-burly. 'Beryl, this is our new Constance. Please get her dressed.'

The girl opened her mouth as though to protest, but then appeared to think better of it and instead levelled her gaze towards me, giving me a look of extreme disapproval. 'Come on, then,' she said, turning on her heel and marching towards a row of partitions made of black drapes.

As I trotted behind her I said, 'We haven't met. My name is — '

'Costume is in there,' she interrupted testily, pulling open one of the drapes. 'Get a move on, then.' With that, she spun around again and strode away.

Oh, the insolence of youth.

The drapes had done their job well, making the changing area so dark that I could barely read the label marked *Constance* on the ornate dress I was expected to wear. The darkness had also made me unaware that there was another in the dressing area, until a sudden movement alerted my attention.

'Good heavens, you startled me!' I told the figure in what appeared to be a long red dress. Only on closer inspection did I realize that I was sharing the dressing room with a man! He was elderly, crouched and bearded, and clad in a long red robe. The Cardinal Richelieu, no doubt. 'I am sorry, I thought I was alone,' I said. 'My name is — '

'Of little concern to me,' he finished for me in a croaking voice, then limped off towards the opening in the drapes.

'Well, I never!' I called after him, but he was already gone. The major requirement for working in motion pictures, it seemed, was a rude disposition!

Since the dressing room (*cell* might be more accurate) appeared to offer all the privacy of Victoria Station, I decided I had best change as quickly as possible. I slipped off my green velveteen dress and donned the costume, which fit reasonably well, then stepped out into the light to await further instructions.

I was soon called to take my place in a tableau that also included the Queen, King, Cardinal (who dourly answered to the name Mr. Faversham), Musketeers, and Harry as the Musketeers' servant. Stepping into our midst, Mr. Johnson explained the scene, which consisted of my removing the Queen's diamond necklace and handing it to her with a curtsey, while she in turn offered it to a kneeling D'Artagnan, as all others reacted. We rehearsed the action, after which Mr. Johnson once more stepped forth.

'When you present the jewels, Lady Ashford, make sure you pause and hold them out in front of you like this,' he said, taking the necklace and demonstrating the way he wanted it displayed for the camera.

'See how I'm catching the sunlight in the stones? Do it like that.' Then, handing the necklace back to her, he said, 'All right, let's try it,' and took his place behind the camera, while Beryl, still in a sulk, watched from the side.

So it went for the entire morning, with one tableau after another set up, explained, rehearsed and then photographed; though how it could be pulled together into a cohesive story was beyond me. Perhaps that was not necessary in moving pictures. After a meagre lunch, which was assembled by the scowling, drudge-like Beryl, the afternoon was spent setting up a sword fight, which for some inexplicable reason was taking place between D'Artagnan and the Cardinal. Had Mr. Johnson even bothered reading Dumas?

When the afternoon light became too dim to continue, we were called into a brief meeting to discuss the scenes that would be photographed on the morrow, after which we were dismissed by the producer.

'So tell me, Amelia,' Harry said as we made our way to our dressing closets, 'what did it feel like to hoist a fortune?'

'What do you mean?'

'The Queen's necklace.'

My confusion must have shown on my face, because Harry exclaimed: 'Gor, ducks, you mean you didn't know it was the real thing?'

'Harry, are you telling me that those were the Ashford Diamonds?'

'Right enough.'

'You were certainly right about Mr. Johnson's taste for realism,' I gasped.

'Oh, it's not just that,' Harry said. 'It's part of Mr. Johnson's publicity strategy. See, the audience in America ain't going to pay to see Maurice Denby or Ralph Faversham, or yours truly, but they *will* pay to see the Ashford Diamonds. In a sense, they're the real stars of the picture!'

I was still trying to absorb this revelation as I entered the dressing area, where another, more sinister surprise awaited me. Pinned to my velveteen dress was a hastily scrawled, unsigned note that read: *If you know what is good for you, get out and do not come back!*

I read the note over and over again, foolishly looking for some inner meaning that was not evident in the terse words; but there was none. There was only the threat — and not a veiled one at that!

What was I to do? I could not solicit advice from my husband, since he was away. I suddenly realized there was one man in London to whom I could turn, as uncomfortable as I might feel doing so. But discomfort or no, I had made up my mind. After changing back into my dress I made my way across the green to Wakefield Street, where I hailed a cab to take me to 221b Baker Street.

'He's not returned yet, dear,' I was told by Mrs. Hudson, Mr. Holmes's long-suffering landlady, upon inquiring after him. 'But seein's how it's you, I don't suppose he'd mind if I let you in to wait for him.'

I agreed to wait, but then almost changed my mind when she opened the door to the cluttered, smoky hovel that the great detective called home. Since papers were strewn over every piece of furniture, I remained standing until I finally heard the urgent footsteps outside the door and was greeted by the sight of Sherlock Holmes roaring into the apartment like a train emerging from a tunnel.

'Mrs. Watson,' he said, rushing past me

and beginning to rummage through the pile of papers that covered his work desk. 'Mrs. Hudson warned me that you were here, though you could not have chosen a worse time to come. I am very busy.'

'And I am rather distressed, Mr. Holmes,' I said, holding the note out to him. 'I received this today.'

Seeing that I was not about to leave, he snatched the paper out of my hand with a sigh of impatience. 'It seems you have offended someone. Imagine that,' he commented dryly, with what I read to be a trace of amusement on his face.

I strenuously protested my innocence and gave him a quick history of my recent involvement with the motion-picture company, concluding with the appearance of the note. 'I am asking you what I should do, Mr. Holmes.'

'My advice, Mrs. Watson, is to do exactly what this note exhorts,' he replied, handing the slip back. 'Do not continue to associate with these people. Actors are a notoriously unstable breed. Who knows what might happen?'

'But — '

'Be so good as to close the door behind you on your way out,' Holmes said, waving me away and turning back to his papers. Close the door I did — with a slam loud enough to be heard in Calcutta.

After finishing a light supper I prepared for bed, my thoughts never very far from the mysterious and threatening note. It had to be the work of that wretched girl Beryl, who had taken an immediate dislike to me for some unfathomable reason, and I vowed to have it out with her the next day. Do not come back, indeed!

★   ★   ★

When I arrived at the glass house the next morning, I saw a small army of uniformed policemen traipsing around the building. The actors, still in their street clothes, were being kept in a herd by two of the constables, while a smallish man in a bowler hat and mackintosh was questioning Mr. Johnson. Naturally, I rushed up to find out what was going on.

A sergeant suddenly stepped in front of me. 'Pardon me, ma'am, do you have a connection with this moving picture?'

'Yes I do,' I replied. 'What on earth has happened?'

'The inspector will take your statement. Stand over there, please.'

As I took my place with the other actors, I could not help noting that the previously pleasant Lady Ashford was not amused. 'Harry,' I said, sidling up to him, 'what is going on?'

'Mr. Johnson arrived this morning and found Beryl Hunter dead. Shot through the heart, she was.'

'Beryl? Why would anyone shoot Beryl?'

'That's what the coppers want to find out. They say we have to wait here 'til they talk to all of us, even her ladyship.'

My attention was suddenly drawn to the covered figure being carried away on a stretcher by two constables; and more specifically, to the pattern of the cloth that was hanging down from under the blanket. I broke away from the group and dashed to the stretcher.

'Excuse me,' I said, 'but is that the victim?'

'Aye,' murmured the constable at the front.

'Could I ask you to pick up the blanket?'

'Here, now!' a voice said from behind, and I turned to see the inspector hurrying towards us. 'Who are you?' he asked me. 'And what's all this about?'

'My name is Amelia Watson, and I — '

'Any relation to Dr. John Watson?' he interrupted.

'Yes, he is my husband.'

'I see,' he said, thoughtfully. 'I've worked with him and Mr. Holmes on a couple of cases. I'm Inspector Laurie of Scotland Yard; perhaps he's mentioned me.'

'No, he hasn't, but how do you do,' I said.

'Hasn't mentioned me, eh?' the inspector muttered, seemingly disappointed. 'Well, no matter. Now then, why did you stop my men from taking away the body?'

'I would like to examine what the victim is wearing.'

The inspector's eyebrows shot up at this request, but he complied without another word, lifting away the blanket himself. I saw what I needed to see, and at the same time felt a chill. Beryl was then recovered and carried away.

'What were you looking for?' the inspector asked.

'She is wearing my costume,' I said.

'So?'

'So perhaps that bullet was meant for me.'

'For you? Do you know of any reason why someone would want to kill you?'

'No, of course not, but yesterday I did receive this.' I showed him the threatening note.

'Hmmm. Well, I can't say whether your fears are grounded or not; but if I were you, I would do just this note advises: go home and don't come back. Just tell the sergeant where we can reach you before you leave.'

After providing the desired information, I turned and started to walk back across the green. Soon I was joined by Harry.

'I'm so sorry, ducks,' he said. 'I feel like I got you all mixed up in this.'

'It is hardly your fault, Harry.'

He shook his head. 'It's a mess, though, ain't it? Gor, poor Beryl. She wanted to be up in front of the camera with the rest of us so bad she could taste it, but she just didn't have the stuff.'

I stopped walking. 'Harry, what are you saying? Beryl wanted to act?'

'More than anything else, I think. And to his credit, Mr. Johnson gave her a tryout, but the results . . . Well, you know, there's good actors — you 'n' me, for instance; then there's passable actors like old Faversham; and then there's duckies and blokes what have no talent.'

'And that was Beryl?'

'Well, even that's being generous,' Harry said. 'As far as talent goes, that poor girl was in debt. She couldn't act, so Mr. Johnson made her the company runner. She did whatever needed to be done.'

Suddenly the motivation behind the threatening note became clear. 'That would explain Beryl's animosity towards me,' I said. 'When your first actress dropped out, Beryl must have thought Mr. Johnson would give the role of Constance to her. But then I showed up out of nowhere and snatched the part away from her. The note was her way of getting rid of me so that she could once more claim the part for herself. Obviously, she thought the note had worked, which is why she was wearing my costume.' That was all well and good, but it still did not resolve the disturbing question of whether the bullet had been meant for me.

'Amelia, you've shipped out and left me at the dock,' Harry said, his face the very picture of comic puzzlement. 'What are you talking about?'

'Oh, nothing Harry,' I said, smiling at his expression. Even when he was not trying to, Harry could make me laugh. Changing the subject, I asked, 'What do you suppose is going to happen now? Will the production continue?'

'I wish I knew,' he sighed. 'Nick Johnson is a keen one for angles, but I don't think he counted on this kind of publicity.'

To take our minds off the present, we reminisced about better days until we had arrived at the omnibus stop. There I bid Harry a fond goodbye and started the journey home.

Since I had anticipated being gone for the entire day, I had given Missy, our maid, the day off; so it was to a quiet, empty suite of rooms that I returned. Not feeling particularly hungry, I took down my favourite volume from the shelf and settled into the armchair, relishing the chance to forget my own problems amidst the travails of Amy Dorrit and her impoverished father. But awash in the brilliance of Mr. Dickens, my own mind began to work more clearly.

Granted, my thoughts were not so much formulating answers as raising questions, and big ones. The biggest of all, of course, was who had killed Beryl; and even more importantly, *why*? The notion that I had been the intended victim faded away as I remembered Harry's comment that Beryl had been shot through the heart, which strongly suggested that the murderer was facing her. Even clad in my costume, I could not imagine anyone mistaking Beryl's size, colouration and features for mine — a fact that only reinforced the poor girl's delusion that she would ultimately be cast in the part of Constance for the remaining photography; for any audience would surely realize the role was being played by two different women.

At that moment something flashed through my mind like a streak of lightning; something that did not make sense, yet at the same time made a great deal of sense. At once a few of the loose threads began to tie themselves together, but only a few. I felt certain that the key to Beryl's murder was still inside the glass house, and I was pretty sure I knew exactly where it was hidden. I paced the sitting room for the best part of an hour to give the police enough time to vacate the crime scene, then set out once more for the glass house.

The structure looked deserted when I arrived, though I walked completely around it, just to make sure. But as I reached out to turn the knob on the door, a hand touched my shoulder.

I gasped and spun around, only to see Harry Benbow standing behind me. 'Harry, you frightened the next five years out of me!' I cried. 'Why are you still here?'

'Got no place else to go,' he said. 'I've just been walking around, thinking about Beryl.'

'As have I, and I believe I might be able to shed some light on this puzzle. But first I would like to get back inside the stage. Do you suppose it is locked?'

'Only one way to find out.'

Fortunately, the door of the glass house had no lock. Squeaking it open, I called 'hello' repeatedly, but received only silence in reply. Satisfied that the glass house was empty, I stepped inside, beckoning Harry to follow, and headed straight for the moving-picture camera.

'Do you know how to open this thing?' I asked him.

'Oh, you can't, it'll ruin the filum.'

'Only if there is any film inside.' I examined the camera from every side but could not identify any kind of release lever or button.

'What are you doing, Amelia?'

'Harry, at this moment I am praying that I am right. One, two, *three*!' On three, I pushed the camera as hard as I could, knocking it off balance and sending it crashing to the floor. Upon impact the box broke open — but instead of spilling out ribbons of film, a glistening strand fell to the floor. I reached down and carefully picked up the silver necklace containing the Ashford Diamonds.

'Gor, I don't believe it!' Harry said, eyeing the jewels.

But then a third voice echoed through the structure: 'I wish you hadn't done that.'

Stepping inside the glass house, armed with a revolver, was Nick Johnson. 'Throw me the diamonds,' he demanded, and there was nothing I could do but comply.

'Mr. Johnson, what is this all about?' Harry panted, raising his hands.

'As you have obviously realized, Miss Pettigrew, an empty camera is the perfect place to hide stolen jewels. Who is going to look inside, for fear of ruining the film? But I'm curious; before I kill you, tell me how you figured this out.'

In a shaky voice I said: 'Yesterday you told me that if the camera were to be opened you would lose all the film you shot the day before. Then you proceeded to photograph an entire second day's worth of tableaux without running out of film. Although I know very little about photography, common sense told me that this camera either contained an incredible amount of film, or none at all. And the only possible reason for the camera containing none at all was that it was being used as a hiding-place for something else.'

'But I saw Lady Ashford wearing the diamonds this morning,' Harry protested.

'I imagine what we saw was a glass replica. Isn't that right, Mr. Johnson?' The American nodded. 'In fact, you switched the real diamonds for the fakes right in front of us, didn't you, when you were demonstrating to Lady Ashford how to hold the necklace up to the light?'

'You amaze me, Miss Pettigrew.'

'My name is Mrs. Watson,' I said with all the defiance I could muster. 'And I also imagine that Beryl somehow found out about the switch. So you shot her and then told the police that you had found the body.'

'I had to silence her. She was waiting for me this morning, in costume no less, threatening to blackmail me into giving her a role in the picture. The silly little fool never realized that there *was* no picture; it was simply a means of getting close to the Ashford Diamonds. But because of that idiot girl and the police, I have already missed my ship, and I cannot afford any more delays.' He levelled the gun at my heart. 'You first, Mrs. Watson. Then Harry. Goodbye.'

I held my breath, which I feared would be my last, and closed my eyes, seeing only John's face in the darkness. But suddenly the building was filled with a shattering sound as thousands of shards of glass rained down from the ceiling, and a figure in grey dropped down as though from out of the sky, landing directly on the startled Johnson! In the resulting fracas a shot was fired, but it went wild, breaking more glass.

Harry then bravely entered the fray, pouncing on Johnson's arm and managing to wrench the gun from his hand, while the grey man delivered a solid punch to the 'producer's' jaw, rendering him unconscious. Only when the grey man looked up did I see, much to my surprise, the ancient face of Faversham, the dour actor playing Richelieu.

But that was nothing compared to my surprise when the man stood to his full height, peeled away the face and hair of the old actor, and revealed himself to be *Sherlock Holmes*!

'Once you have recovered from your general shock, Mrs. Watson,' he said, wiping away the remainder of his make-up, 'be so good as to fetch the police.'

Within the quarter-hour the team of constables, once more under the direction of Inspector Laurie, had returned and were leading the shackled form of Nick Johnson towards a police wagon. After interviewing Mr. Holmes, Harry and myself for nearly another quarter-hour, the inspector pronounced himself satisfied. I, however, was not.

'Mr. Holmes, why did you not reveal yourself to me in the first place?' I demanded.

'I could not take the chance,' he answered, casually dabbing his handkerchief at a cut on his hand, the result of crashing through the glass roof. 'I had spent a month trailing Johnson and was getting too close to him to risk discovery. It was imperative that my disguise remain impenetrable; and since you had managed to see through one of my masquerades in the past, you were the most serious threat to that imperative, which is why I was forced to leave you that melodramatic warning.'

'*You* were the one who left the note?' I cried.

'Not that it did any good,' he said, 'even when you came to me that evening and gave me the chance to reinforce the message in person. I thank the heavens, madam, that most criminals are not so difficult to dissuade as you are.' Then, giving one of his electric smiles, Holmes bid us both good day and disappeared across the green of Coram's Field.

'Gor, I didn't know you were married to *that* Dr. Watson!' Harry said.

'There is a lot you do not know about me, Harry,' I replied. 'But if you will permit me, I will try to fit in as much as possible tonight at dinner at Simpson's. It is my husband's favourite eating house.'

Since we both knew that I would be paying, Harry was gallantly reluctant at first, but I managed to persuade him. As it turned out, the dinner at Simpson's was made even more delicious by Harry's company, and we promised to stay in touch.

Two restful days later, John returned home with encouraging news regarding the health of his fellow Northumberland Fusilier. 'How I missed you, Amelia,' he said affectionately. 'I hope things were not too dull while I was away.'

'Oh, you know how it is, darling,' I replied. 'Once more, I managed to survive.'

The Adventure of the Bramley Court Devil

'John, I would like to swap seats,' I informed my husband, hoping to escape, or at least diminish through distance, the highly annoying snoring sound that was coming from the elderly man seated to my right.

'As you wish, Amelia,' John replied, rising and allowing me to inch past until we had exchanged places; though it quickly became evident that not even objectionable sounds would ruin his enjoyment of the evening, which was the first he had taken away from his writing desk in heaven knew how long.

I, however, was feeling less expansive, since the accomplishment of having pulled him away from the recording of his exploits with Sherlock Holmes had been tempered by his insistence on choosing the play we would attend. That, in short, was why we were squeezed into a capacity-filled house at the Monarch

Theatre, waiting for the curtain to rise on a penny-dreadful melodrama titled *The Torments of Honoria*, rather than seated in the newly opened New Gaiety Theatre, eagerly anticipating its premiere presentation, *The Orchid*, which had been my recommendation.

As it turned out, Honoria was not to be alone in torment. I too was suffering at the hands of the playwright, whose clichéd and hackneyed dialogue was delivered by the actors with a note of apology in their voices. John, on the other hand, sat raptly through every painful line and absurd convolution of the plot, so much so that I finally abandoned the play entirely and began to watch his reactions, which were far more entertaining.

But my attention was ultimately forced back to the action on stage by the sound of a fearsome shriek, followed by a collective gasp from the cast. I watched with new interest as the actors, moving as one, stepped back to allow a strange, dishevelled man to stagger centre stage.

'The Devil!' he cried, a look of abject horror on his face. 'I seen the Devil in

Bramley Court!' The man then collapsed onto the stage and lay still. The actors looked back and forth at one another, vainly trying to figure out what to do; and within seconds the curtain rapidly descended.

A low murmur rippled through the audience, most of whom, like me, had realized that something was dreadfully wrong; though a smattering of applause was offered by those who had not. My husband, alas, was in the latter grouping.

'Ripping!' he declared, clapping enthusiastically. 'What a way to end an act! It is a mark of a skilled author to concoct such a singular surprise.'

'I have a feeling that even the author might be shocked by this turn of events,' I replied.

'Really, Amelia, you cannot mean to say that you believe this man was not somehow part of the drama,' he protested. But before we could debate the issue further, a lone figure had appeared on stage in front of the curtain, his hands raised in an appeal for silence, which he quickly got.

'Is there a doctor present?' the man called out in a thin, reedy voice.

'Great Scott,' John muttered, then leapt to his feet, shouting, 'Yes, I am a doctor!' Squeezing past the other theatre-goers to get to the aisle, he dashed to the stage, while I followed as rapidly as my dress would allow.

'I am Dr. John H. Watson,' he told the man on stage, who in turn identified himself as the stage manager.

'And I am Mrs. Watson, here to assist my husband,' I hastened to add; and we were quickly ushered through the curtain. Breathing in the unique aromas of stage paint and make-up, I was suddenly transported back to a wonderful time, long since past, when I was an actress (albeit an amateur one). I probably would have stood transfixed indefinitely had not the voice stage manager whinnied: 'Is he all right?'

I then became aware that John was kneeling down beside the prone figure — a red-faced, middle-aged man whose clothing betrayed signs of overuse. After checking the man's pulse at the neck and then the wrist, John gently lowered the limp hand to the floor. His expression told all. 'This man is dead,' he said.

'Dead?' the stage manager croaked. 'How?'

'Difficult to tell,' John responded. 'I can find no evidence of injury, though judging from his state when he collapsed, I would say it is possible that he died of fright. Did he work here?'

'No, I have never seen him before,' the stage manager replied. 'The doorman said he rushed in from the street, and before he could be stopped, found his way onto the stage. We have already sent someone to fetch the police. Would you be good enough to stay until they arrive, sir?'

'Of course.'

'Thank you. I must go and inform the audience that the performance is cancelled. I doubt any of us are in a state to continue.' Wringing his hands, the man disappeared through the curtain to make his announcement, which was greeted with a chorus of groans.

We did not have long to wait for the

police. Even before the last patron had filed out of the theatre, a familiar figure in a mackintosh and bowler hat appeared backstage. 'Why, Dr. Watson,' he said. 'Are you now finding out about crimes before the police? Or are you simply causing them yourself?'

In unison, John and I both said: 'Inspector Laurie, how do you do.'

'Ah, Mrs. Watson, you are here as well,' the inspector said. 'It has been a while.'

John regarded us with a quizzical expression. 'A while? I was not aware you two even knew each other at all.'

'Oh, yes,' the inspector went on. 'Mrs. Watson and Mr. Holmes were helpful in cracking a case a while back.'

'When was this?'

'You were out of town, darling,' I said, adding weakly: 'I will explain it later.'

'So, Doctor, what have we got here?' the inspector asked; but before John could recount the dead man's dramatic appearance, the harried stage manager had reappeared, saying: 'I would like to be able to dismiss the cast, Inspector, unless you need them.'

Inspector Laurie turned to the actors, who were huddled upstage. 'All right, listen up,' he commanded. Then, pointing down at the sprawled figure, he asked: 'Has anyone here ever seen this man before?'

Each actor in his or her turn responded in the negative, with the manager concluding: 'He is not one of us, Inspector.'

'All right, they can go,' Inspector Laurie said. Turning back to John and me, he added: 'I would like to hear more from you two, if you don't mind.'

'I wish there were more to report,' John said. 'At one point in the play the man dashed on stage — '

'To the obvious consternation of the actors,' I interjected.

' — and he shouted something about having seen the Devil, then fell down dead.'

'The Devil, you say?' the inspector said.

'On my honour,' John replied.

'No, no, what I mean is, you're sure he said 'the Devil'?'

'I believe his exact words were, 'I seen

the Devil in Bramley Court',' I said. Immediately the inspector's face darkened.

John, however, seemed oblivious to this sudden change of mood. 'If you ask me, this is an open-and-shut case,' he stated.

'Indeed, Doctor?'

'Absolutely. Given the facts as we know, I think I can explain what happened. By the condition of this clothing, which can best be described as shabby, we can deduce that this fellow is of limited means. The redness and slight swelling around his nose reveals him also to have been a heavy drinker, and therefore probably not a man who looked after his health. It is safe to assume that he could have had a serious heart condition and not even known it.

'This evening, he must have drunk enough to bring on some form of the *delirium tremens*, which in his mind manifested as the Devil himself. Panicked, he ran through the streets screaming blue murder, and into the first open door he came upon, which would have been the backstage entrance of this theatre. As he staggered out onto the stage, his mind was further confused by the lights and the sudden appearance of an audience; and so he made his dramatic statement and then expired.'

'A very interesting theory, Doctor,' Inspector Laurie said. 'However, that does little to explain the four other people who have reported seeing a demon of some sort in the area of Bramley Court over the past three nights.'

A half-hour later the three of us sat ensconced in a booth at Simpson's in the Strand, where Inspector Laurie, having confessed to working through supper, was devouring a plate of pork loin and roasted potatoes.

'You don't really believe the Devil has arisen in London, do you, Inspector?' I asked.

'I'm but a simple copper, Mrs. Watson, not a theologian,' he replied. 'But at this moment, I'm not sure what I believe.'

'Perhaps you should seek Holmes's opinion of this business,' John suggested.

'Aye, and so I tried. I called on him yesterday morning, but his landlady said

139

that he is off somewhere on a case.'

This news brought a frown to John's face. 'That's odd; Holmes usually notifies me when he is leaving town.'

I suspected that I might have had something to do with the great detective's sudden coolness toward his bosom friend, since the last time I had seen Mr. Holmes I had managed to cause him some considerable discomfort in front of the most illustrious witness in the Empire. Deservedly so, I might add. But that was no reason to punish my husband.

'Do not worry yourself, darling,' I said. 'You know Mr. Holmes and his whims better than anyone.'

'Yes, I suppose so,' he replied. 'But in his absence, Inspector Laurie, perhaps I could help you.'

The inspector looked up from his plate. 'Help me in what?'

'Help you investigate this singular mystery.'

Dabbing at his mouth with a napkin, the inspector said, 'Look, Dr. Watson, it's not that I don't value your advice; but I'm hardly in a position to let an outsider get involved in the case.'

'Outsider?' John bristled. 'Really, Inspector. I have been called in to assist the police on many occasions.'

'Still, darling, it is not your responsibility,' I said. 'After all, the police are paid to look for demons in dark alleys.'

'True enough,' Inspector Laurie said, 'and there are few places in London as dark as Bramley Court. It's the centre of a tight, dirty little maze of narrow alleyways — the perfect hiding place for a criminal on the run. They can't demolish the place fast enough for my liking.'

'Demolish it?' I said.

'Aye, as part of the Kingsway improvements. A few years back they cleared out the Clare Market slum to make room for the new thoroughfare between High Holborn and the Strand.'

'Yes, I remember,' John said, nodding.

'Yet for some reason they left Bramley Court, the worst part of the district, standing. Maybe they didn't need the land yet, or some such. But whatever the reasoning behind it, it is coming down now, and I say good riddance.'

Inspector Laurie drained the remainder of his coffee cup, then dug a shilling out of his pocket and plunked it on the table. 'Well, I had better get back to see what the lads have discovered. If you do happen to hear from Mr. Holmes, let me know.' He then rose, jammed his bowler back on his head, bid us good evening, and took his leave.

John spoke no more about the bizarre occurrence in the theatre, either in the restaurant or on the way home, which was not an encouraging sign. I have known my husband long enough to know that when he does not speak, he is ruminating; and such ruminations too often lead to his taking rash action.

My feelings of apprehension were heightened when the yellow glare of the streetlamp outside our home in Queen Anne Street revealed that his face had magically shed itself of years, and the distinguished-looking grey streaks at his temples had miraculously regained a natural brown hue — a remarkable transformation that occurred whenever my husband was excited by the prospect of a case. But with Mr. Holmes out of the picture (or perhaps *because* of that), I knew that he was contemplating striking out on his own, despite the admonition from Inspector Laurie. My role in this scenario was becoming clear: whatever it took, I must keep him out of harm's way.

I said nothing until the proper moment, which came shortly after the church tower had tolled eleven. Still dressed, John took up his hat and coat once more and announced, 'I do not feel sleepy, my dear. I believe I will go out and walk for a bit.'

'What a delightful idea,' I countered, reaching likewise for my hat and quickly pinning it on. 'I shall accompany you.'

'Uh, no, there is no reason for that,' he replied. 'I mean, there is no reason for you to tire yourself.'

'Oh, I am not tired either,' I lied, 'and you know how much I enjoy dank, foggy nights.'

For several moments we stood facing each other like fighters in a ring, each knowing exactly what the other one was plotting. Finally John said: 'You know,

Amelia, you cannot stop me from going to Bramley Court.'

'I am quite aware of that, dear — just as *you* must be aware that you cannot stop me from accompanying you. Having settled that at last, shall we go?'

As we sped through the night streets of London in a chilly hansom cab, I startled myself with the realization that, far from preventing my husband from carrying out a rash and possibly dangerous act, I was actually looking forward to approaching the precipice with him. I wanted to know what lay behind the stories of the Bramley Court Devil, and the thought of poking around until I found out gave me a slight tingle of pleasure. Heavens, what on earth had happened to the staid, respectable doctor's wife I used to greet each morning in the mirror? I tried to contain my growing excitement lest John discover it, at which point all would be lost.

Before long we arrived at Holofernes Street: a dark, eerily lifeless passageway that, according to our driver, was the entrance to the district. It quickly became clear that it was also as far into the slum as he would take his steed.

The street was dotted with piles of earth and broken stone that spoke of the demolition that had already begun. Inspector Laurie had not been exaggerating in likening the quarter to a maze; and as we proceeded through it, a thick yellow fog began to envelop us, making it even more difficult to find our way through the web of ancient courts. My squirrel coat was little protection against the night chill, which, along with the bleak setting, sent a shiver through me.

'Perhaps this was not a good idea,' I offered.

'Perhaps you are right,' John answered. 'The fog has become so dense there is little we can see. Let us go back home.'

But then a third voice, coming from behind us, shattered the quiet. 'I thought I had made it clear that this was no place to be at night,' it declared.

John quickly spun around, taking me with him; and with some effort I was able to make out the form of Inspector Laurie, flanked on either side by a constable.

'Mind telling me what you two are doing here?' he asked.

'Simply taking a walk,' John said brightly, as though our presence in this dismal quarter was a commonplace occurrence.

'Of course,' the inspector said sceptically.

'But since we are here,' I added through chattering teeth, 'have you learned anything more about the man in the theatre?'

The policeman sighed. 'I suppose it won't hurt to tell you. Seems his name was Muggerage; at least, that's what was written on the inner band of his hat. He most likely lived around here, since he frequented a local gin shop over on Earls Court. According to the other pub flies he was a quiet sort; stayed pretty much to himself, particularly after his wife disappeared.'

'Disappeared?' I said.

'Run off with a sailor, so the gossip goes.'

'Anything else you can tell us?' John asked, in tones that sounded so much like those of Sherlock Holmes that I did not know whether to laugh or cry.

The inspector did not reply. Instead his attention was focused on the sound of running footsteps, which appeared to be coming toward us. 'Who's there?' he called out, and soon the figure of a very young constable appeared out of the fog. 'Oh, it's you, Bingham. What have you got?'

''E's gone, sir!' the young constable blurted out.

'Who is gone, Constable?'

'The dead man, sir.'

'*What?*'

'We called for the wagon, just like you said; but when we went back into the theatre to get him, he was gone.'

'Don't tell me you left the body alone!'

'Well, sir, I . . . that is . . . all of us reckoned that he was not in so much of a hurry to go somewhere that we could not leave him where he was for a second or two.'

'In other words, long enough for someone to slip in and remove the body right out from under your noses.'

'Yes sir,' the young constable said bleakly. 'What should we do now, sir?'

'Search the area, man. Look for anyone who appears to be carrying a large object. If you see two people together, stop them just as a matter of course. I want the body found, Constable!'

'Yes sir!' The younger policeman then disappeared into the yellow mist.

After instructing the two constables who were accompanying him to join in the search, Inspector Laurie turned to John and me. 'As for you two, I trust I can rely on your silence regarding this. It's bad enough that the papers are going to get wind of this Devil's business, but I don't need them to start trumpeting the notion that an eyewitness rose from the dead and walked away.'

'You may be assured, Inspector, that I have no interest in providing the newspapers with sensational information,' John said. 'However, if a reporter were to approach me directly with a question relating to the rumoured disappearance of this Muggerage, it would hardly feel right to lie about it. Unless . . . '

'Unless what, Doctor?' the inspector enquired, so tensely that I feared John had overstepped his bounds.

'Unless we were to be taken into your full confidence regarding this case and allowed to see it through to its conclusion.'

Inspector Laurie sighed deeply. 'All right. Given this turn of events, I suppose it won't really hurt to have another brain involved. But mind you, this is strictly unofficial.'

After receiving our assurances of cooperation, the inspector released one of the constables to escort us out of the maze and stand watch over us until we were safely inside a cab headed for home.

Given the evening's excitement, I had no difficulty sleeping that night. When I arose the next morning, I found that John was already dressed and filling the day room with pipe smoke, and pacing in a circle while pondering the problem. The copies of the *Times*, the *Sphere*, the *Graphic*, the *Illustrated London News* and the *Police Gazette* that were spread across the table-top gave evidence to his having gone out while I slept. True to the inspector's predictions, the morning papers were, in a matter of speaking, full of the Devil.

'Have you arrived at any deductions, darling?' I asked, fanning my way through the smoke.

'Only that this entire matter is most puzzling,' he said, stopping his pacing and facing me. 'The problem I am having, Amelia, is in trying to decide whether this is simply a case of natural death with bizarre overtones, or cold-blooded murder.'

'Heavens, what makes you suspect murder?'

'The disappearance of the body. Why else would it have been taken before it could be thoroughly examined, if not to cover evidence of foul play?'

'I cannot imagine. Unless, of course, this Muggerage had something valuable on his person.'

John nodded. 'That had crossed my mind as well. But if that were the case, why steal the entire body? I confess, Amelia, that I am absolutely confounded.

There are enough strange occurrences to fill three such cases, and yet no clues! At least none that I took the time to search for. I could positively kick myself for not examining the body more closely while I had the chance. His clothes, even his shoes, might have revealed something.'

'Darling, I doubt even the man's shoes would have given up the secret of the apparition in Clare Market. Unless, of course . . . '

'Unless of course what?'

'Unless he sold his soles to the Devil,' I said, unable to stifle a schoolgirl giggle. Alas, John was not in the mood for levity, and soon left for his surgery. After finishing my toilette, breakfasting, and giving Missy, our maid, her instructions for the day, I departed for the Monarch Theatre, in hopes of obtaining a refund on the price of our tickets for the abortive performance of *The Torments of Honoria*.

I managed to arrive at the theatre before the box office had opened and, having nothing better to do, I strolled along its portico, watching the comings and goings of the citizenry of London. My attention was soon focused upon one man who appeared to be running across the green toward the theatre. Pulling a notepad and pencil from his coat pocket, he dashed up the steps and darted inside. Curious, I followed him and soon found myself as one of an assembly of people gathered in the lobby. Everyone but I was scribbling on a pad — reporters, undoubtedly — and the focus of their attention was none other than 'Honoria' herself, now out of costume and make-up (and I hope no one will think it mere *meowing* if I report that this 'ingénue' will never see forty again).

'It was the most dreadful experience,' she cried dramatically. 'I fear I shall faint once more at the memory of it! He charged onto our stage like a madman, shrieking as though the harpies themselves were in pursuit, made his ghastly declaration, then . . . fell. Save for the cry of the Congolese Wild Man I once encountered at the circus, I have never heard such a sound emerge from a human being.'

And so it went, until I decided I had had enough of these fevered histrionics and slipped back through the door.

Once I had finally obtained my refund, I decided to spend the afternoon shopping, or at least walking idly from one shopfront to the next, while continuing to turn over in my mind the particulars of this puzzling case. After a time, though, my mind was as weary as my feet, and, being nearly four o'clock, I decided to stop at Buszard's and treat myself to a pot of tea and a scone, after which I hired a cab to take me home.

Much to my surprise I found that John had already returned from his surgery and was poring over a new collection of newspapers. 'Oh, there you are, my dear,' he said absently. 'I had no appointments this afternoon, so I took the opportunity to leave early.'

'Is the Devil still front-page news?' I asked, slipping off my shoes.

'Even more so. Listen to this: 'Stories of the horrible apparition that has become known as the Bramley Court Devil have spread so rapidly that many members of a crew working to widen the road through the area have refused to return to the site.' Inspector Laurie will not be pleased to hear that.'

He read in silence for a few more moments, then exclaimed, 'Great Scott, listen to this: 'Miss Evangeline Currey, who claims to have seen the Devil Thursday night while walking to her home, describes the creature as standing eight feet tall and bearing the head of a goat, from whose mouth emanated flames.''

'Good heavens!'

'It certainly sounds fearsome, though I think we can allow for some exaggeration, if not outright delusion.' Picking up the latest edition of the *Times* from the top of the stack, John glanced down its front page before settling on a column near the bottom. 'Ah, here is yet another eyewitness account,' he said. ''Mr. Battison informed the Metropolitan Police of seeing a creature some eight feet in height, with the head of a goat and fire spewing from its — ' Good Lord, the descriptions are identical!'

'What does that mean, John?' I asked.

'It means that we can no longer hide behind the notion of delusions. Something is really out there, Amelia — but what? What on earth could possibly fit this description? Certainly not a man. No man stands eight feet tall.'

At that moment Missy entered the room to ask: 'Will you be taking dinner in this evening, sir? Mum?'

'Yes, though later, Missy. I am not very hungry now,' I replied.

'You're not feeling ill, are you?' asked John, ever the concerned physician.

'I am fine, but I stopped at a tea shop near Oxford Circus while I was out, so — ' I stopped suddenly and placed a hand to my forehead. 'Oh!'

'What is it, Amelia? Something has come to you, hasn't it?'

'I think I know what kind of man stands eight feet tall and breathes fire,' I said. 'But how can it be — ? Missy, please leave us now.'

Once she had exited the room I told John of my suspicions, tenuous and improbable though they were; nay, *impossible*, since my theory had in it a flaw so enormous as to virtually negate it. But with growing excitement, John theorized a solution of his own that completely eradicated the flaw.

'We must contact Inspector Laurie at once!' he cried.

'Indeed, John,' I said, 'and then we must return to Clare Market and do whatever it takes to raise the Devil.'

The sky was darkening by the time we reached Holofernes Street. The unearthly quiet of the now-empty neighbourhood was disturbed only by the sounds made by John, myself, Inspector Laurie, and the small army of policemen he had assembled.

'For the time being I will accept your theory as a possibility, Mrs. Watson,' the inspector was saying. 'But *only* as a possibility, and a slim one at that. And only because we do not have any better — '

'Shhh, Inspector, listen,' I interrupted, suddenly aware of a strange noise. 'Do you hear that?' From somewhere came a muffled thump, followed by a scraping sound; then the thump again, then the scraping, over and over.

'I hear it,' John said. 'It sounds like someone digging with a pickaxe.'

'It seems to be coming from over there, perhaps from inside that house,' I said. Slowly, we advanced on a dark, dilapidated building that, except for the noise that was indeed originating inside, appeared to be deserted. Inspector Laurie silently motioned for his force to surround the house, and a half-dozen hardy souls proceeded down the foreboding alley that bordered the hovel. Once they were in place, he marched to the front door and pounded on it.

'Open this door by order of Scotland Yard!'

The digging sound stopped immediately.

'Whoever is in there, I order you to come out!' the inspector shouted again, and after a suitable period of silence, cried: 'Very well, we are coming in!'

Two brawny constables threw themselves against the front door, which proved to be stronger than it looked. They were still at it when the first shouts came from the back of the house.

'Mary, Mother of God!' cried one policeman as he ran past us and down the court.

'I believe we have succeeded,' I said, trying to sound calm; but it still took all my nerve to face the ghastly apparition that now lumbered down the alley. The eyewitnesses' descriptions were horribly accurate: the top of the goat-thing's head stood even with the roof of the house, and a flare of yellow fire was indeed spurting from its mouth. Its body was obscured by a billowing black drape that glistened in the light of the fire.

'Good Lord!' Inspector Laurie cried, as John simply stood gaping at the thing. I, however, sprang into action.

'Amelia, let the police handle it!' John shouted as I charged the demon, running headlong into its black garment, groping blindly for the plank of wood I felt certain would be there. It was buried within the black cloth; but once I had located it I grasped it tightly with both hands and pushed as hard as I could. With an angry bellow, the figure toppled forward and landed with a thud. Upon impact, the goat's head flew off and the black drape caught fire. The man inside it all frantically wrestled his way out of it, then spit a mouthful of oily liquid onto the ground. Leaping to his feet, he looked around for an escape route, but quickly realized he was surrounded.

'That was quite a show you put on, sir,' Inspector Laurie said as two constables rushed in to grab the man and hold him fast. 'I think some of my men will be having nightmares for the next week.'

'Damn your lousy peeler's hide,' cried Mr. Muggerage, very much alive. 'How'd you know it was me?'

'Since that was deduced by Mrs. Watson, I shall let her tell you.'

'The person who really deserves the credit is the leading actress at the Monarch Theatre,' I began. 'In speaking with reporters, she likened your cry as you ran onto the stage to that of a circus wild man — a remark that rested innocently in my memory until jarred loose by trying to imagine what kind of

159

mortal could stand eight feet tall and breathe fire. It was then I was struck by the only possible answer: a man with the skills of a stilt-walker and a fire-eater — in other words, a circus or side-show performer. Since you had already been linked to that vocation by way of your dramatic cry, you became in my mind the prime suspect. But there was one obvious problem with that theory: you were dead, or so we thought. It was my husband who solved that particular conundrum.'

'When Amelia confessed to me her suspicions,' John said, 'I suddenly recalled a trick my friend Sherlock Holmes learned in Tibet, whereby through deep concentration he can slow his pulse to the point of imperceptibility. It was reasonable to assume that the same trick, or something like it, could be in the repertoire of a side-show performer.'

'It also served to explain the disappearance of your body,' I continued. 'When no one was looking, you simply got up and walked away. The one mystery that remains, Mr. Muggerage, is why you have done all this.'

'You're so bleeding smart, you tell me!' he snarled. 'You're just as bad as my wife, you are. It was her what got me sacked from the circus, damn her! And damn you, too, you bloody bitch!'

I confess that his speech shocked me, as it would any lady of refinement; but I was completely unprepared for what happened next. Before any of the policemen could stop him, John rushed the man, crying, 'How dare you!' and struck him with his fist, knocking the villain unconscious with one blow! I had often heard John speak of a youthful temper — 'keeping a bull pup' was his term for it — but I had never before witnessed it.

It had obviously taken Inspector Laurie by surprise as well, since he stood open-mouthed for a few moments, then recovered enough to order his men to take the limp figure away. 'This time, don't let him get up and walk away from you,' he commanded.

'Inspector,' called one constable, who was emerging from the house, 'I think you'd better have a look inside.'

161

Using police torches, we made our way through the dark, filthy structure until we came upon a sight that filled me with revulsion. Dug into the earth under the floor was a shallow grave containing human bones, loosely laid in a tattered woman's garment. 'I have a suspicion that Mrs. Muggerage did not run away with a sailor after all,' I said, a lump rising in my throat.

Inspector Laurie knelt down by the grave. 'Muggerage must have realized that the workmen who demolished the house would uncover the body as well, so he created the Bramley Court Devil, hoping that the ensuing panic would stop the work, at least long enough for him to remove the evidence himself.'

'You almost have to admire the man's inventiveness,' John said.

★   ★   ★

Two nights after the horrible discovery in Bramley Court, we found ourselves once more enjoying the convivial hospitality of Simpson's with Inspector Laurie: a fitting place to bring the investigation that had begun there to a close.

'There is one thing I do not yet understand, Inspector,' I said. 'Why did Muggerage rush on stage that night and then fake his own death?'

'I asked him that very thing myself,' Inspector Laurie said, digging into his sherried trifle. 'It seems that his first appearances as the Devil frightened those who saw them, but they failed to spread the kind of panic he was looking for, chiefly because we managed to keep the reports out of the papers. So he had to go public, so to speak, which he did by bursting into a crowded theatre and planting the rumour of the Devil to several hundred people at once. As for his death act, that was simply a means of escaping detection. Even the Yard stops short of questioning dead men.'

'Ingenious,' John said.

'Aye. His only mistake was in choosing the very theatre you two were attending.'

'For that you may solely thank my husband,' I said.

'I do have to confess, though, Mrs.

Watson, that I was prepared not to believe your theory. Tying it all back to Muggerage, just on the supposition that he was once in the circus, was a mighty leap of logic.'

John smiled at this. 'As Holmes is fond of saying, when you have eliminated the impossible, whatever remains, however improbable, must be the truth. But I must commend you, Inspector, at having wrenched the entire story out of this blighter. He seemed to me to be the uncooperative type.'

'Oh, that was no trouble, Doctor. We told him that either he talked to us or we'd let you come down and take another poke at him.'

Taking up John's hand, which was still red and sore from defending my honour, I batted my eyelashes and twittered, 'My knight in shining armour!' in such fashion as would have done Honoria proud.

The Adventure of the Retiring Detective

'Good God!' my husband cried, clutching the pages of the evening *Times* so tightly that they threatened to rip.

'What is it, John?' I asked, concerned and a little frightened by the intensity of alarm in his tone.

The look of shock remained on his face as he read from the paper: ' "The body of a woman found floating in the Thames near the Hungerford stairs has been conclusively identified as Mrs. Irene Norton, the former Irene Adler of the European operatic stage. The police have ruled the death a suicide.' I cannot believe it!'

'How terrible. Did you know this woman?'

'Not really, though I have long felt as though I did. Irene Adler was entangled in a singular puzzle some years back involving the King of Bohemia. She was the only woman ever to beat Holmes at his own game, and as a result, he became fascinated by her. He always referred to her as *the* woman and kept her picture in a place of honour in his room.'

I vaguely recalled hearing some mention of *the* woman in the past, but until then, I never knew to whom it was referencing. 'I must confess, darling,' I said, 'that I never pictured Mr. Holmes as one capable of schoolboy crushes.'

'Oh, it was hardly that. It was her intellect and spirit he admired. He never expected to see her again; indeed, she had vowed never to return to England. Now this. Poor Holmes; how perfectly terrible for him.'

I might have thought it perhaps a bit more terrible for the victim, but I said nothing. If being the wife of Dr. John H. Watson has taught me anything, it is that his odd friend Sherlock Holmes was always at the top of his consideration.

'The poor fellow must be distraught,' John continued. 'He might even be tempted back onto the needle. I must away to him at once.' Rising from the chair, he rushed to the coat rack by the door.

'Must you go now?' I called after him, but I could see the determination setting in his face and realized there would be no stopping him. 'Very well, if you must run out now, I shall accompany you,' I said, hastening to get my own coat and hat.

'There is no need for you to go, Amelia,' he protested, throwing on his coat.

'While I do not have your experience with Mr. Holmes, John, I have known him long enough to realize that he would reject outright a blatant offer of sympathy and assistance, even from you. However, if we were to both appear at his door, saying that we had been walking in the neighbourhood and decided impulsively to drop in for a friendly visit, he would be less likely to erect a guard around himself.'

Grudgingly, John agreed.

The night was chilly and the cab was draughty, but fortunately Mr. Holmes's refuge in Baker Street was not very far from our own home in Queen Anne Street.

'I have this strange sense of foreboding,' John confessed as we walked up the familiar stairs to Mr. Holmes's first-floor rooms. While I do not know what he was steeling himself for, I can state with certainty that the sight that greeted us at the door came as a shock.

The woman who opened the door to John's former apartment appeared to have just emerged from her bath. Her long auburn hair was still set and the only covering on her body was a man's dressing gown! The scent of shag tobacco that permeated the garment identified it as belonging to Sherlock Holmes. But what on earth was this wet, unclad woman doing wrapped inside it?

'I . . . I . . . I am s-sorry to disturb you,' John burbled out, directing his gaze towards his shoes.

'No disturbance at all, Dr. Watson,' the woman said, her voice betraying American roots. 'Won't you come in?'

John suddenly looked up. 'Do we know each other?' he asked, studying the woman's face, which was radiantly beautiful even without any trace of cosmetics. His jaw then dropped as he cried: 'Great Scott, you are Irene Adler! I recognize you from that photograph of Holmes's. But the news-papers reported that — '

'Let us discuss it inside, please,' she entreated. 'The open door is creating quite a draught.'

Once we had entered the previously male-only domain, Irene smiled at me and said: 'You must be Amelia. Sherlock told me that Dr. Watson had married again. Speaking of which, Doctor, I am Irene Norton now.'

'And where is Mr. Holmes?' I asked, returning the smile, equally wondering the whereabouts of Mr. Norton.

'He is out, but he mentioned that you would most likely be contacting him as soon as you saw the fraudulent report he planted in the newspapers. Please make yourselves at home while I go change,' she said, exiting into a side room.

'But that is my bedroom,' John muttered, his eyes following her through the door.

'*Was* your bedroom, dear,' I said, patting his hand.

'Surely she cannot be living here!'

The opportunity to find out came

quickly, as Sherlock Holmes breezed through the door a few seconds later.

'Ah, Watson, how good to see you,' he said perfunctorily, tossing his hat on a battered hat rack in the corner and draping his coat over the back of the settee. 'And Mrs. Watson as well,' he added, a degree or two more coolly. Then a phantom smile broke across his face.

'Your look of Puritanical disapproval, Watson, tells me that you have already encountered Irene. I assure you that the reason for her presence is as simple as it is necessary,' Holmes stated, stuffing tobacco into a sooty clay pipe that looked as though it had recently been excavated from a Bronze Age dig. 'I desire to keep her alive.'

The woman in question returned to the room, dressed now in a simple white shirt-waist and dark grey skirt, her still-damp hair combed down straight and draping her shoulders. I noticed that she wore no rings on her hand, even though she continued to use the name Mrs. Norton.

A widow, I guessed. What I could not discern was why she should be having such difficulty staying alive as to require the services of a detective.

'Sit down, please,' Holmes said, lighting the pipe as he draped his long frame across a battered armchair. 'I would offer you coffee, but I have sent Mrs. Hudson away. As startled as you seemed to be by Irene's presence, Watson, Mrs. Hudson would have been scandalized to the point of evicting me from the premises. I intend to keep her away until this dark business has been concluded.'

'What dark business?' John asked.

'Perhaps I should let Irene herself explain,' Holmes said, leaning back and closing his eyes while the pipe continued to smoulder in his hand.

Mrs. Norton turned to us and began: 'My husband, Godfrey, died two years ago. He was, as you may recall, Dr. Watson, a lawyer. After a number of years on the continent we resettled in America, where Godfrey quickly became one of Boston's most successful attorneys, catering mostly to the cream of New England society. But being a foreigner on American shores himself, he was rarely able to refuse an appeal for help from another foreigner, even if they possessed no resources to pay him. It was through one such case that we first learned the truth about Randolph Harding Bowers.'

'Who is Randolph Harding Bowers?' I enquired.

'I am sorry, I had forgotten that the name means little in England,' she replied. 'In the United States, however, he is as well-known as T.R. himself.'

I looked to John, still puzzled. 'T.R.?' I wondered aloud.

'Theodore Roosevelt, the American President,' Holmes interjected, the first indication that he had remained awake since Mrs. Norton began speaking.

'To directly answer your question, Mrs. Watson,' Irene Norton said, 'Randolph Harding Bowers is a man of almost incalculable wealth and power. He either owns or is partnered in a good many of the nation's mining and manufacturing companies. It was one of his factory employees who contacted Godfrey, seeking his help; and after hearing the man's strange story, Godfrey began an investigation of his own, speaking with other workers in Bowers's factories and mines. Not only were these interviews done at his own expense, but they were accomplished with a secrecy and cunning that would have done Sherlock proud.'

Sherlock. That was the second time the woman had regarded Mr. Holmes in a very familiar fashion, and I began to wonder anew about her presence in his rooms in a state of undress, only to push the thought out of my mind as too immodest to contemplate.

Mrs. Norton continued: 'Over the period of one year, Godfrey had spoken with dozens of Bowers workers, men and women, and in every case had received the exact same story: Randolph Harding Bowers was not an employer in any accepted sense of the word, but rather a slave-holder.'

'A slave-holder?' I cried. 'I thought that sort of thing had been abolished years ago.'

'Indeed it was,' she replied. 'Unfortunately, Randolph Bowers is not a man to let the law stand in his way. Using a series of agents placed throughout Europe, Asia and Australia, Bowers would find people who desired to immigrate to America and offer them transport, lodging and a job once they had arrived. Most of these unfortunates told Godfrey that it sounded like a dream come true. But once the would-be immigrants arrived in America, secretly, via a shipping line owned by a friend and confederate of Bowers's, they were immediately put to work in a Bowers mine or a Bowers factory and were provided with a filthy cot in an overcrowded bunkhouse and meagre board in lieu of wages.'

'The unmitigated villain,' John huffed. 'Did not anyone object?'

'If anyone tried, they were threatened with deportment to lands other than their own. If anyone talked of escape, they were detained in one of Bowers's makeshift jails. If anyone actually tried to escape, they would invariably be caught and . . . '

'Go on,' John said.

'Their bodies would be placed on

public display as an example to the others.'

'Good God!'

'Was this man Bowers responsible for your husband's death as well, Mrs. Norton?' I asked.

'Please call me Irene,' she responded with a smile, which I returned. 'And no, he was not. During the year in which he was investigating Bowers, Godfrey began to take ill. He tried to hide his condition from me, but it soon became painfully clear that he would be denied the time to use the evidence he had uncovered to fight this dangerous man. On his deathbed, Godfrey handed me his notebook, containing notes of all the interviews he had conducted as well as the names of the other wealthy businessmen involved in the scheme. My last words to my husband were that I would somehow find a way to bring Randolph Harding Bowers down. Now, of course, it has become all the more imperative.'

'Why is that?'

'Bowers has announced his plans to

run for the governorship of Massachu-
setts, the avowed first step in his quest for
the presidency itself. Through his network
of spies, he has managed to find out
about Godfrey's investigation, and he
knows that I am holding the evidence that
would ruin him. In short, Mrs. Watson
— Amelia, he is on to me. I know for a
fact that I have been followed for the past
three months.'

'Cannot you go to the American authorities with your evidence?' John asked.

'Powerful men tend to have powerful
friends, Dr. Watson,' Irene replied. 'I
honestly do not know whom I can trust.
But my immediate problem is that I
cannot at this moment lay my hands on
the notebook. Godfrey's final instructions
were to send it to an old friend of his,
Simon Belfont, here in London, with the
instructions that the notebook be depos-
ited into a private bank vault, and the key
be sent back to me in Boston. He felt it
would be safer if the notebook was in a
different country, out of Bowers's reach.

'Unfortunately, I fear he underesti-
mated the length of the man's arms. Once

I realized that I was being watched, my only thought was to retrieve the notebook, my only true weapon against Bowers and his army of thugs, as soon as possible. I booked passage to England under an assumed name, hoping to be out of the country before my actions were discovered. Alas, I was not successful.'

'Which is why Holmes planted the suicide notice in the papers,' John said.

'Precisely, Watson,' Holmes said, suddenly bolting upright in his chair. 'And with the complete approval of Scotland Yard, I might add. If Irene's pursuers believe that she has been driven to take her own life, their own investigation will be rerouted, and that will allow us enough time to overcome the major obstacle in this case.'

'Which is?' John asked.

'Finding the notebook, of course.'

I was becoming confused, which was not an uncommon occurrence in the presence of Mr. Holmes. 'But didn't you just say the notebook was in the bank vault?' I queried.

'Indeed I did,' Irene replied, 'and so

179

indeed I thought it was. But when I went around first thing this morning and offered my identification as well as the key, the vault proved to be empty. The notebook is missing.'

'But surely this can lead to only one conclusion,' John cried. 'The fellow to whom you sent the notebook never put it in the vault.'

'*Of course* that is the only conclusion, Watson! A child of seven could see that!' Holmes said brusquely, and again I wondered how John had managed to endure his friend's condescension for so many years. 'The bigger problem,' the detective went on, 'is that Simon Belfont appears to have disappeared as well.'

'What is to be done, then?' John asked.

Pacing back and forth and puffing smoke like a nervous locomotive, the detective replied: 'Mrs. Watson, I must ask you to take Irene in as a boarder for the time being. She will be safer there than here.'

I looked to John, whose expression indicated total agreement and willingness, before answering, 'Very well. Missy, our maid, is away visiting family, so Irene can stay in her room.'

'It is settled then,' Mr. Holmes said. 'As for you, Watson, I will require you to be here at Baker Street.'

'I am at your call, Holmes,' John said, and I opened my mouth to protest, but shut it again, knowing that when he was on a case, nothing on earth would stop him; least of all me.

'Now, Watson,' Mr. Holmes went on, 'please remove your hat and coat and give them to Irene, so that anyone who might be watching from outside will see Dr. and Mrs. John H. Watson leave, the same as they arrived.'

'But if someone really is watching, don't you think they will be able to tell the difference between Irene in an overcoat and my husband?' I protested.

'Not if the two of you call upon the acting skill I know you both to possess in order to fool them,' Holmes said, permitting himself a smile. 'You must go now. Watson and I have a great deal of work to do.'

'Be careful,' I begged my husband, and

was surprised to hear Irene bid the same to Sherlock Holmes.

Clad in John's coat and hat, and walking with robust movements, Irene Norton presented a much better image of a man than I would have suspected possible. The biggest problem in the deception was the fact that she stood several inches shorter than my husband. But reaching up on her tiptoes, while I crouched as low as I possibly could and still maintain a normal appearance, we were able to maintain the illusion of reversed height. We stood in the doorway to 221b until a cab appeared within hailing distance, which Irene signalled. When it stopped, I put my arm through hers, as I normally would my husband's, and together we entered the cab.

Once we were on our way, Irene appeared to relax. 'I truly appreciate your help, Amelia,' she said.

'It seems little enough,' I replied, 'if this man Bowers is really that dangerous.'

'If not stopped, I believe Randolph Harding Bowers could become the most dangerous man in the world. But if anyone can thwart him, it is Sherlock.'

'You know, Irene, it has struck me that you always call Mr. Holmes by his Christian name.'

'A display of comfortable familiarity about which you are curious?' she replied, a wry smile on her face.

'Guilty, m'lud,' I answered, which made her laugh.

'Perhaps someday, after we have become even closer friends, I will tell you all about it.'

The cab soon pulled up to the kerb in front of our house in Queen Anne Street, which, after paying the driver, we quickly entered. Once inside, however, I stopped, suddenly alarmed.

'What is it?' whispered Irene, seeming to sense my concern.

'The lamp in the sitting room has been turned off,' I whispered back. 'I know we left it on. Someone has been here.' It was then I heard a muffled thump coming from somewhere inside our home. 'They are still here!' I shouted, grabbing Irene's arm and wrenching the door open. 'We must get out!'

But the next sound I heard caused me to stop, and I turned back as a weak, pain-filled voice called: 'Dr. Watson, is that you?'

'Whoever it is, he sounds injured,' Irene said.

'Let us go and see, then,' I said, withdrawing the sturdiest of John's walking sticks from the umbrella stand and holding it in front of me as a weapon as we entered the sitting room. In the darkness I was able to make out a shape sitting in John's chair.

'Do not move; I am armed,' I told the shape as I made my way to the lamp, clicking it on.

As soon as the room was illuminated, the man in the chair cried: 'For God's sake, turn it off! The light — it's like daggers in my eyes!'

I gasped at the terrible sight of the strange man, whose bearing was hardly that of a ruffian, but whose face was covered in bruises, one of which all but closed his right eye. I switched the lamp off, casting the room once more into darkness.

'Who are you?' I asked.

'My name is Belfont, Simon Belfont,' he muttered, then turned in the direction of Irene. 'Are you Dr. Watson?'

'No, I am Irene Norton, Godfrey's wife,' she replied, throwing off John's coat and hat.

'Oh God,' he moaned, 'it is because of you that I've been held captive and tortured.'

'Tortured?' I cried.

'Being tied up in a chair . . . blind-folded . . . beaten . . . In my book, that is torture.' The poor man actually produced a small, sardonic laugh as he added: 'But it was not *my* book that the men wanted, was it?'

Irene suddenly became alarmed. 'The notebook! You haven't given it to them, have you?'

'No. It is in a safe place. For now, at any rate.'

'Please, tell me everything,' Irene beseeched.

'Yes, including how you ended up in my sitting room,' I added.

'In a way, I have no one to blame but

myself,' Belfont began, his voice now somewhat stronger, but still laboured. 'About a week back I noticed an advertisement in the agony column of the *Times*, which read: 'Mrs. G. Norton, recently returned from America, seeks what she has lost. Come in person.' And then it gave an address.'

'I put no such advertisement in the papers!' said Irene.

'I know that now,' Belfont continued. 'The address in question turned out to be a vacant building, so I turned around and came back. Only later did I realize that the summons was a trap, and that the empty building was being watched for whoever might turn up. From that moment on I was aware of someone following me, watching me. I saw the man repeatedly on the street. He was not very proficient at his task. I quickly realized that I was not the subject of this bizarre game, but rather Godfrey's notebook, though I was determined not to lead my pursuers directly to it. Fortunately, John Hemmings, the manager of the bank, is also a member of my club. I convinced him to open the vault with the bank's key and deliver the notebook to me, which he did.'

'That is why the box was empty when I got there,' Irene said.

Simon Belfont nodded. 'I had just managed to get it to its hiding place when I was abducted. My watchers must have got impatient and decided to take more drastic measures. There were two of them, and they succeeded in beating the information out of me, or so they thought. I told them of the bank vault and added that I did not possess a key, all of which was perfectly true.'

'How did you get away?' I asked.

'Like most brutal men, my captors were quite stupid. I convinced them that I would act on their behalf and get the key from Mrs. Norton when she arrived. In return, they loosened the rope holding me. Once they had fallen asleep, I worked my way out of my bonds and escaped. My first thought was to go immediately to Baker Street to see Sherlock Holmes. But upon arrival in the cab, I noticed that the same man who had been following me was standing across the street, watching the house. I told the driver that I had changed my mind. It was then that I discovered that cabmen know everything there is to know about London.'

'How so?' I enquired.

'The fellow quite frankly informed me that I seemed more in need of a doctor than a detective, and offered to take me to the home of Dr. John Watson, where I would have access to both. So here I came. I apologize for the means of entry,' the poor man said, gesturing towards the window, which I only now realized was open, 'but no one came to the door.'

Irene leaned close to him. 'Mr. Belfont, please tell me where you have put the notebook.'

My eyes had become accustomed to the darkness, and I was able to make out a tiny, grim smile that cut through the pain etched on the man's face. 'The one place too obvious to be considered,' he said. 'Columns . . . that is my revenge. I was duped through the agony column. Let us see if they find their way through *my* columns.'

'But where, Mr. Belfont, *where*?'

The man's smile quickly dissolved into a grimace of pain, and he grabbed his head with both hands and moaned, then fell limp.

'We must get him to a hospital,' I said. Leaving Irene with the stricken man, I rushed outside to try and find help, which soon arrived in the form of a police constable. I gave him only the barest of facts regarding the presence of a strange injured man in my sitting room, and before long an entire troupe of policemen arrived at our home. An officer who identified himself as Sergeant Potts supervised the transport of the unconscious Mr. Belfont to nearby Middlesex Hospital. As they were leaving, I asked the sergeant to please contact Sherlock Holmes regarding the matter.

By the time the excitement was over, it was nearly eleven o'clock and I felt exhausted. Irene, however, still looked alert, if somewhat troubled. I practically fell into John's armchair, which still carried the warmth of our unfortunate visitor. 'I shall never be able to under-stand how John thrives on this sort of thing,' I muttered.

Irene appeared deep in thought. 'What do you suppose he meant by 'columns'?' she asked.

'It sounded like delirium to me.'

'True, but the other thing he said, something about hiding the notebook in a place too obvious to be considered, seemed quite lucid.'

'Until the poor man recovers, I fear we shall never know what he really meant.' I rose from the chair and yawned. 'I am sorry, Irene, but I simply must get some sleep. Our maid's room is through there. It is not large, but the bed is comfortable and bedding clean.'

'Thank you, but I think I will stay up a bit longer.'

I could see that finding Simon Belfont, only to have the information he possessed slip away, was greatly troubling Irene, but I was in no condition to sit up with her and keep her company. Upon bidding her goodnight I headed for the bedroom, and minutes later slipped in between the sheets on our bed, which was destined to remain cold and lonely for the rest of the night. The last conscious image my mind produced before surrendering to sleep was that of a row of Ionic columns, a picture planted in my head by the unfortunate Simon Belfont.

★ ★ ★

It is difficult to say how long I had been asleep prior to bolting upright in the bed, my head spinning, and any hope of further sleep chased away like a fox pursued by hounds. I dashed out into the sitting room to find Irene, still dressed, asleep on the sofa. I shook her gently. 'Irene, wake up.'

'Hmmm?' she muttered, opening one eye, then another. 'Amelia, what is it?'

'Irene, Mr. Belfont was not delirious,' I said. 'He was telling us exactly where the notebook is hidden!'

We could not, of course, act upon my intuition at that moment; but after a sleepless though hardly unpleasant night, given the company, Irene and I set out that morning, far too anxious to be tired. Taking the omnibus to Great Russell Street, we were soon standing in front of one of the city's most notable classical façades.

'It is in there, behind the columns,' I said, staring at rows of them.

Irene smiled. 'The perfect place to hide a book,' she said. 'Our Mr. Belfont was quite clever.'

Without another word, we entered the British Museum and made our way towards the great library. If my supposition was correct, it would not take long to find the notebook. Rushing to the 'N' section, the two of us followed the names printed on the spines of the books until we arrived at one slender volume which had no printing at all.

'Here it is!' Irene cried, only to be *shushed* by a group of readers nearby. Almost reverently, she pulled the treasure from the shelf, where it had been hidden in plain sight. Flipping through the pages drew from her a sigh of relief. 'It is all intact, every page,' she said. 'We must away to Baker Street now.'

'No, Irene,' I said. 'Look over there.'

A rough, villainous-looking specimen was standing in the entrance to the library, regarding us with grim amusement.

'Another one over there,' Irene whispered, drawing my attention to yet another man whose gaze never left us. All in all, there were four of them positioned throughout the book-filled rotunda. 'God in heaven!' she cried out. 'Is there no escape from them?'

The sudden rise in her voice prompted one elderly scholar, who was perusing volumes nearly as dusty as himself, to *ahem* rather pointedly before informing us, 'This is a library!' I was about to point out to him the utter redundancy of his statement, when I saw a beatific smile break out on Irene's face.

'A library, sir?' she said demurely, stepping towards him. 'I thought it was a concert hall.' And with that Irene Norton, *née* Adler, opened her mouth and produced the most beautiful contralto tones I have ever heard. I then remembered the planted suicide notice John had read which had named her as a star of the European operatic stage.

What her selection was from I could not say, though it was performed as though she were singing for her life (which, in a sense, she was). While a few of the library patrons appeared to appreciate the unexpected concert, there were more like the pinched man standing next to us who seemed to list making noise in the British Library as one of the primary qualifications for perdition.

'Please, madam,' the man shouted in spite of himself, 'be quiet!'

'Oh, be quiet yourself!' I shouted back. 'You are interrupting the concert!'

It was not long before the police constables arrived, which I had come to realize was the purpose of Irene's impromptu aria. As the first policeman strode through the reading tables towards us, she suddenly stopped singing and levelled a finger at one of our burly surveillants, shouting, 'There he is, Constable! That is the man!'

Startled, the man turned and started to dash out, but was stopped by another constable. The others in the library followed suit, though I am very glad to say that none made it past the line of officers.

Irene and I were, of course, escorted out under police guard as well, and I daresay that we did little to help our cases by giggling like a pair of naughty schoolgirls all the way to Bow Street. By the early afternoon, though, we were released, thanks to the depositions of the men who had been assigned to watch us, the evidence of the notebook, and the testimonials on our behalf from John and Mr. Holmes, who had been sent for as soon as we reached the Magistrates' Court. But our freedom was predicated upon the solemn vow that we must never again create a public row in the British Museum.

On the way back to Baker Street, I enquired after the condition of Mr. Belfont.

'He is rather severely concussed, though he should recover fully with time,' John responded. 'In fact, we had hopes he would be well enough within a few days to at least to inform us as to the whereabouts of the notebook.'

'The two of you saved us that trouble,' said Holmes, whose Sphinx-like countenance made it impossible to tell whether he was annoyed by our actions or amused.

John continued: 'Once the recovery of the notebook looked imminent, Holmes took the liberty of contacting an American justice official, who is at this moment sailing to England in order to receive it in person. He assured us that, based on your husband's testimony, Irene, Bowers is as good as imprisoned.'

Upon hearing this, Irene muttered something so quietly that I was unable to distinguish it. At first I thought it might have been a prayer, but upon reflection a few days later I realized that it must have been: 'I have done it, Godfrey.' By then, though, everything had changed.

The four of us spent the rest of the day together, and it was very strange to see Mr. Holmes in purely social circumstances. He remained quiet, if not boyishly bashful throughout, though I detected enough subtle looks and smiles exchanged between Irene and him to make me wonder anew what had once passed between them that they were not revealing.

It was dusk by the time we returned to Baker Street. We had just exited our cab and watched it pull away from the kerb when the sounds of another approaching carriage filled the street. 'Mrs. Norton!' a voice called from behind us, and Irene turned around.

'Irene, no!' shouted Mr. Holmes, and John and I spun around to see a dark brougham with a man leaning from its window. With a lightning-fast snap of his hand the man flung something, though I could not see what it was. The carriage then sped away and disappeared into the night.

The next thing I heard was John shouting: 'Great God!' And for a moment everything seemed to be happening at once, but slowly. I heard John once more, this time saying: 'Irene, do not try to move, we shall get an ambulance.' Only then did I see a sight that tore my heart from my body. Irene Norton was lying on the pavement, her simple dress coloured by her own blood. John was kneeling beside her, his skilled surgeon's hands hovering helplessly over the knife that was embedded in her chest.

'We will get you help,' he was saying.

'No, it is too late,' she whispered. With obvious pain, she raised her head and looked toward Mr. Holmes, who now knelt beside her as well. 'I shall soon see Godfrey,' she panted, 'and I shall tell him that I saw you again, Sherlock.' A slight, knowing smile then graced her lips. 'But I shan't tell him everything.'

Her head fell back down on the pavement, and John slowly stood up, removed his coat and draped it over her.

Sherlock Holmes slowly rose, his gaze still cast down on the body. When he finally looked up, I saw more pain reflected in his eyes than I believed possible for a man to bear. 'I should have foreseen this,' he said in a flat, dead voice that caused me to shiver even as I wept. 'I swear to you, Irene, that I shall not rest until I have found the man or men responsible for this. This night, Sherlock Holmes shall cease to exist, except to bring this ring of killers to justice. Watson, I shall require your help for this.'

'Anything, Holmes, anything,' John choked.

'As soon as this notebook is handed to the American authorities, I will leave Baker Street. You will inform the public that I am no longer available to act as a consulting detective.'

'What shall I say?'

'Say anything, Watson. Say I retired to the country to keep bees. I do not care. I leave it in your hands.'

'Where will you go, Mr. Holmes?' I asked, sniffing and sobbing like a child.

'Everywhere. Nowhere. Only by becoming a phantom will I be able to track down the devils who have done this.'

'We will we see you again, won't we?' John asked, his voice unsteady.

'When the need occurs, yes,' Holmes said quietly. 'Until then, Watson, goodbye.' He turned and stiffly strode to the door of Baker Street, his thin hands clenched into ivory fists. But at the stoop, he turned back. 'One more thing you must do, Watson,' he called.

'Yes, Holmes?'

'You must protect your wife and keep her safe. If you do nothing else, old friend, do that.' Sherlock Holmes then entered 221b and closed the door.

I have no doubt that John and I shall indeed see Mr. Holmes again, though when and where I cannot say. Yet whenever I think of him — which is surprisingly often — I find myself hoping that his self-imposed quest will not be a long one, and that he will manage to find peace within himself and return to being the same brilliant, righteous, infuriating, and ultimately all-too-*human* being who, in a strange way, captivated the brave and loyal heart of my husband, Dr. John H. Watson.

And in an even stranger way, captured a little bit of mine as well.

The Adventure of the
Japanese Sword

'What do you say we take a walking tour of San Francisco?' my husband entreated. 'We should experience the city. I understand there is an eating house here that actually serves buffalo meat.'

'You cannot be serious, darling,' I moaned, falling back on the bed. After an entire week spent aboard ship followed by six more torturous days covering the American continent by train, I was in no condition to go traipsing through a strange city, particularly one that requires the traipser to be half mountain goat. And having seen a buffalo from the window of our train, I did not even want to contemplate dining on one. 'Can't we stay in this evening, John, just the two of us?'

'But this is such a grand city, Amelia,' he continued, displaying the unnaturally youthful cast that comes over him when he is truly excited. 'I do not wish to waste a minute in seeing it again.'

'Again?' I asked, raising my head from the pillow. 'You have been here before?'

'Oh yes, years ago, before my army service. Did I not tell you?'

'I think not. You know, dear, sometimes I worry that you deliberately hide details of your early life from me.'

'Nonsense. You are not coming, then?'

'Please, John, I must rest,' I begged. 'Perhaps by tomorrow I will be better able to conquer the colonies.'

John left the hotel shortly thereafter to drink in the city before going to inspect the lecture hall where Friday evening he would be regaling the American multitude with his adventures in the company of Mr. Sherlock Holmes (and how deliciously ironic that I had foresworn an early career on the stage only to marry a man who would embrace one in his middle years).

No sooner had he gone than I fell into a deep sleep, from which I was rudely awakened a mere hour and a quarter later by a pounding at the door. Rising with effort, I discovered the caller was a young hotel bellboy brandishing a brown envelope.

'Letter for you, ma'am,' he said, thrusting the envelope in my hand. 'I also have a message from a Dr. Watson.'

'Oh?' I yawned. 'What is it?'

'He put a call through to the desk downstairs and said to tell you that the sponsors of his speaking tour have arranged a dinner with a representative of the mayor's office. He asks that you join him at eight o'clock at Dominico's restaurant in New Montgomery Street.'

After acknowledging the message, I waved the lad away and shut the door. I still did not feel like emerging from the comfortable hotel room, but if John thought it was important enough to send for me, I suppose I should at least try to make the effort to go. I then turned my attention to the envelope which was addressed to my husband, though I did not think he would mind if I opened it.

Instead of a letter, it contained a photograph of a woman wearing a bridal gown seated next to a man in formal wear, obviously a bride and groom. I stared at it uncomprehendingly at first, but then the image registered in my brain with searing clarity. The man in the picture was very young but his face was unmistakable. I was looking at an old wedding photograph *and my husband was the groom*! I had seen a photograph of Mary, John's late first wife — or at least the woman I had been told was his first wife — and this creature was not her. Was I indeed the *third* Mrs. John Watson?

As I groped for understanding, I flipped the photograph over and found on the back a handwritten note:

My dear Johnny,

How long it has been! I read of your impending return to the city and decided that I must see you again. You will find me at the Hurley Hotel in Post Street.

Yours, Constance Adams

Johnny? I read the note over and over and over again, feeling increasingly numb. How could he have kept a secret such as this from me? Now shockingly awake, I was determined to find out. I could hardly confront my husband in a restaurant, surrounded by the benefactors or our visit here; so, quickly working to make myself a speck more presentable, I placed the photograph in my handbag and set out to call on this Constance Adams.

As it turned out, the Hurley Hotel was but a few blocks away, a trek that in London would have taken less than a quarter-hour. But in an unfamiliar city, shivering from the damp coldness that was, if anything, worse than London's, and unnerved by the clanging parade of cable-drawn railroad cars that held dominion over the streets, the journey seemed endless. It was with relief that I finally spotted a brass plaque that announced the garishly painted wooden edifice behind it as the Hurley Hotel. I marched in and enquired at the desk (which was manned by a fellow of lackadaisical demeanour) after Miss Adams, and was given a room number on the third floor, which I promptly located.

Bracing myself for whatever unpleasantness might follow, I rapped on the door of room 3-C, but received no answer. I rapped again, this time calling out Miss Adams's name, and was once more greeted with silence, though the door itself budged open.

I stepped inside to find a room that was comfortably furnished, though the solitary wall lamp strained to provide enough illumination. 'Miss Adams?' I called again, but no answer came. Assuming that she had stepped down the hall and would return momentarily, I opted to wait.

A closer examination of the room revealed a bookshelf filled to capacity with volumes that turned out to be elementary readers and school spelling books. Resting on top of the bookshelf was a large sheet of yellow paper on which was printed:

LET YOUR VOICE BE HEARD!
Fight the Union Labour Party and its insidious attempts to rid our fair city of an entire race of noble people who have caused no harm to anyone.

The handbill went on to describe the plight of the Japanese community in San Francisco (which apparently was considerable) and how this Union Labour Party was advocating its complete separation, if not total exclusion, from the city. It was signed *Constance F. Adams, Educator*.

I finished reading the document, which was written with fervour and passion, and then noticed a closed door, which I took to be the entrance to the bedroom. Perhaps she was not down the hall, but sleeping. I knocked lightly and called her name, and when I received no response, I opened the door.

Oh, how I wish I had not.

The horrible sight on the bed made me cry out. Constance Adams (for it surely was her) was laid out on the mattress as though posed, and her simple dress was stained by a dark red pool over the stomach. Next to the body was a very long, slender, slightly curved sword with written characters that I guessed to be Japanese embossed on the handle. I did not need to approach Miss Adams closely to know that she was dead.

I found myself backing, almost involuntarily, away from the scene, out of the room and into the hallway, stopping only when I made contact with another body, one that put its hands on my shoulders!

'Whatsamatter with you?' a rough voice asked and I spun around, finding myself face to face with a coarse-featured man who reeked of alcohol.

'A woman is dead in there,' I said, pointing to the room from which I had just emerged. 'We must notify the police.'

'I'm the hotel detective,' the man replied. 'I'll take care of it.' He lurched past me and entered the room, emerging a few moments later, looking grim. 'Yellow devils,' he uttered.

'I beg your pardon, Mr . . . ?'

'Hanrahan,' he drawled. 'And what I mean is the Japs. They're starting to form criminal gangs just like the Tongs, damn 'em. The Tongs, at least, have the decency just to kill each other and leave the real people alone, but this . . . ' He regarded me with red, watery eyes. 'What's your connection with this, anyway?'

'I came to call on Miss Adams and

found her thus,' I replied. 'Why are you so sure it was the work of a Japanese killer?'

'Because I'm not stupid,' he cried. 'The murder weapon was left right there to tell us who was responsible. The devils want us to know who did it.'

'But why would the very people she was trying to help kill her?'

'Trying to help?' he slurred, looking confused. 'Look, lady, you're talkin' to a former Pinkerton man, all right? I've got this under control, so why don't you just go back to Boston, or wherever that accent comes from, and stay out of my way. Go on, scram.'

It is rare that I am at a loss for words, but the sheer ignorance and rudeness of this man succeeded in robbing me of coherent speech.

I spun on my heel and marched back down the stairs to the lobby and out into the cool night. I continued to walk, propelled onward more out of anger than a desire to reach a destination, and as a result became quite lost in no time at all.

I began to notice, however, that a private carriage had slowed down to stay

211

apace beside me. At first I ignored it, a task that became more difficult when a white-whiskered face appeared out of the cab the window and called in a wheezy voice: 'Would you care to join me inside, my dear?'

'I would not,' I responded.

'I daresay I could make it worth your while,' the man rejoined.

Irate at the implication, I turned and faced him directly. 'And I daresay that I am not what you think I am!' I shouted.

'On the contrary, Mrs. Watson,' came a low, familiar voice, 'I know exactly who you are.'

I gaped at the man, stunned. 'Mister — ' was all I got out before he interrupted me, saying: 'House, Sherrin House of Boulder, Colorado, at your service. Are you sure you won't join me?'

'Indeed, Mr . . . House, thank you,' I said, stepping into the carriage and seating myself next to a white-haired and bewhiskered Sherlock Holmes!

'My compliments on the beard, Mr. Holmes,' I replied. 'Even this close I cannot detect a trace of spirit gum.'

'Nor will you. The hair is all mine. The whiteness, of course, is fabricated. Where might I deliver you this evening?'

I gave him the name of my hotel, which he relayed to the driver, and we set off. 'What in heaven's name are you doing in San Francisco?' I asked him.

'I swore that I would not rest until those responsible for Irene Adler's death have been brought to justice, and I have not. That quest has brought me here. But what of you, Mrs. Watson? I presume you are here with the good doctor, who I see is bringing his rampant storytelling skills to these shores; but that does not tell me what terrible trouble you have experienced this evening.'

'How did you know that?'

'The angry tread of your step, the grim expression on your face, the unconscious opening and closing of your fist. Really, madam, you might as well have been carrying a sign that read: *I am distraught*.'

'I have indeed had a dreadful evening,' I said, telling him of my ghastly discovery in the Hurley Hotel. He frowned slightly upon my description of the nature of

Miss Adams's fatal injury. 'Something about this matter bothers you, Mr. Holmes?'

'The Japanese believe the belly to be the house of the soul,' he stated. 'You have heard of *hara-kiri* — literally, belly-cutting? It is a form of ritual suicide and considered an honourable death. Murder, however, is not an honourable death, but a vengeful one. Given the placement of the wound, I doubt a real Japanese was involved at all. More likely someone attempting, quite clumsily, to make it appear that the murderer was Japanese. But you continue to withhold from me a vital fact regarding this deadly affair.'

'I have told you everything, Mr. Holmes.'

'Except what you were doing in the woman's hotel room in the first place.'

I sighed. 'Very well. I have reason to suspect that the dead woman was in reality John's first wife.'

Surprise registered on the detective's lean, whiskered face. 'Watson mentioned no such affair to me,' he declared. 'He was a bachelor up until the time he met Mary Morstan and remained completely devoted to her thereafter, until she died. This is your destination, I believe.' Mr. Holmes gently prodded, and I numbly stepped down from the cab.

'Mrs. Watson, I beg you not to inform your husband of my presence here,' he said. 'It would only distract him while risking exposure for me. Our reunion will take place soon enough. I must now bid you good evening.' With that, his vehicle sped away into the night.

I made my way to our suite, only to find it a beehive of activity.

'Amelia!' John called as I appeared in the doorway. 'Where on earth have you been? I cancelled the dinner when I received word that you were feeling ill, and came back here, but you were gone. Are you all right?'

'I do not know, John,' I said truthfully.

A uniformed policeman was hovering around the suite, along with a short, boyish-looking man whose face struggled to be seen from under a great shock of auburn hair. 'Is there anything I can do,

Dr. Watson?' he asked, and John introduced him to me as Mr. Bullock, an aide to the mayor of San Francisco, and our escort while in the city.

'There has been a terrible tragedy this evening, Amelia,' John said. 'A woman has been found murdered.'

'How dreadful,' I muttered. 'Have you been called in on the case?'

'Not exactly, Mrs. Watson,' Mr. Bullock answered. 'Your husband's name and information regarding your visit here were found in a notebook in the woman's hotel room.'

'An admirer?' I asked hollowly.

'Someone I knew a long time ago,' John answered with a pained expression.

I was about to enquire further, when Mr. Bullock blurted out: 'You know, Dr. Watson, calling you in on the case is not a bad idea. Perhaps you should go and inspect the murder scene yourself. After all, you are as experienced a detective as any on the force here.'

'You flatter me,' John said, puffing up slightly.

'I wish to go, too,' I stated. 'And please

do not argue, John, since this is obviously the only way we shall be together this evening. Besides, I will be there to comfort you in your loss of an old acquaintance.' Although he regarded me with a quizzical expression, John did not argue.

We journeyed by windy, noisy cable car to the Hurley Hotel, where yet another police officer led us to Constance Adams's room. 'It would probably be best if you did not come inside the room until we get things cleaned up,' Mr. Bullock told me.

I was on the verge of protesting when I noticed the door to the room next to Miss Adams's creaking open. A woman with luxurious blonde hair peeked out and motioned me over. 'What's going on over there?' she asked.

'It seems the woman who lived there has been murdered,' I replied.

Her eyes widened. 'Go on! C'mon in and tell me all about it,' she said, opening the door and pulling me through. Introducing herself as Sally Probert, the woman pressed me for details of the slaying and reacted to each gossipy titbit with a mixture of horror and excitement. For my part, I used this opportunity to find out more about Constance Adams.

'She was a teacher, but not in the schools,' Sally said. 'She taught English to little Japanese kids, and sometimes to their folks. That was kind of a crusade of hers, but it wasn't very popular. A lot of people around here want to run the Asiatics out of town, not teach them to read.'

'So I've gathered,' I said. 'That horrid Mr. Hanrahan seems eager to blame the murder on a Japanese criminal ring without even considering other possibilities. Almost too eager, in fact.'

'Well, I think I would notice a Japanese gang wandering around,' she replied. 'But I haven't seen anybody unusual, except for that workman yesterday.'

'Workman?'

'Yeah, some guy carrying a big long pipe on his shoulder. Big guy. I figured he was here to do a plumbing job or something, but it must've got cancelled, because the water was never shut off.'

The voices from the room next door were getting louder and more animated, so after promising to keep her informed I took my leave of Sally and stepped back into the hallway. As I approached the open door of 3-C I heard a voice shout: 'Would you mind telling me how someone carrying a weapon the size of a Japanese sword could walk right past the hotel detective unseen?'

'They're tricky devils,' slurred Hanrahan, more visibly intoxicated than when I had left him, and who was rigorously being questioned by a plainclothes police sergeant. From the bedroom came two uniformed men carrying Constance's body on a stretcher, and I quickly stepped inside the room to allow them to pass through the door, shuddering as they went by.

'At least tell me the name of the woman you say found the body,' the sergeant demanded. 'You did get her name, didn't you?'

At that exact moment, Hanrahan wobbled his head in my direction. 'That's her right there in the hallway!' he

219

bellowed, levelling a finger at me.

'My wife?' John shouted.

'The man is obviously mistaken,' Mr. Bullock charged.

'What the man is, obviously, is stinking drunk,' the sergeant said. 'Get him out of here and find a charge to arrest him on.'

Another uniformed policeman took hold of Hanrahan and bodily dragged him out of the room and down the hall, the detective's protests trailing behind him like so much smoke.

'I hope you realize, Sergeant Kellin, that Mayor Schmitz will accept nothing less than a full-scale effort dedicated to rounding up the yellow thugs that are responsible for this,' Mr. Bullock declared.

'You may inform his honour that all effort will be made to find *the killer or killers*,' the sergeant replied pointedly.

Mr. Bullock's eyes narrowed. 'It sounds as though you don't believe that the Asiatics are behind this.'

'Motive, Bullock, what's the motive? Tell me that. And then tell me how somebody snuck a three-and-a-half-foot sword through a hotel lobby without anyone seeing it.'

As this argument was taking place, I was inching over to the bookcase, prepared to 'discover' the printed hand-bill that I had noted earlier, but to my surprise I found that the paper was no longer there. I glanced quickly around the room, but it was nowhere to be seen. Had it been deliberately removed to support the presumption of a Japanese conspiracy? And if so, by whom?

I drifted back to the conversation. 'Obviously there is nothing more we can do here,' Mr. Bullock was saying to John. 'Do you require anything else this evening, Doctor?'

'Oh, it seems like a decidedly poor time to ask,' John mumbled.

'Please, Dr. Watson, I am at your disposal. What do you want?'

'I should be grateful for any recommendations of a good breakfast eatery.'

After jotting down his suggestions on a scrap of paper and handing it to John, Mr. Bullock accompanied us to the lobby and engaged a buggy to return us to our hotel room. Once there, I had every intention of confronting John about the photograph; but the events of the day conspired against me, and I was simply too exhausted to pursue the matter. It would have to wait until my mind was clearer.

I arose the next morning refreshed, but also quite ravenous. 'Breakfast is beginning to sound like an excellent idea,' I told John.

'Where is that list of restaurants Bullock gave me?' he muttered, searching through his trouser pockets. 'Ah, here it is.' He handed me the note and I read off the list of eateries, and then stopped cold. I was no longer looking at the writing, but rather the paper itself, which was yellow. Turning it over, I saw letters printed on the back — *ducator* — letters that conveyed no meaning whatsoever, unless one had read the full inscription on the handbill: *Constance Adams, Educator*. It was Bullock who had spirited away the evidence of the flyer, but why?

'John, what do you know about Mr. Bullock?' I asked.

'Very little, except for his work, which

is practically all he talks about,' he answered. 'That and politics, particularly that Labour Party that he and the mayor represent.'

'Labour Party?' I said, suddenly feeling cold.

'Yes, United Labour Party, or some such. 'The party of the working man,' he calls it. Do you know that Bullock claims that virtually every workman in the city belongs to one trade guild or another? Amelia, are you all right?'

I realized I was cradling my head between my hands, trying to keep my mind from spinning away. 'Yes, John,' I said, 'though I fear we must postpone our breakfast and seek out that police sergeant immediately.'

Within the hour, we were sitting in an office at the city's police headquarters and speaking with Sergeant Kellin. 'That is quite a story,' he said gravely, after I had laid out my speculations. 'But what proof is there?'

Unfortunately, none at all, I was about to confess, when Mr. Bullock chose that moment to burst unannounced into the

223

meeting. 'Dr. Watson, Mrs. Watson, I got word that you were down here,' he said. 'Is there anything I can do for you?'

An idea flashed through my head. 'Oh, no thank you,' I began. 'I was just telling the sergeant of the notion that I had this morning regarding the murder. You see, while you were in the rooms of the murdered woman last night, I spoke with her neighbour next door, Sally Probert, who remembered seeing a workman in the building, carrying a length of pipe.'

'So?' Bullock said. 'She probably saw a plumber.'

'But the water had not been shut off, she said. Obviously there was no plumbing work done, so what was the man doing there? Then I remembered that Sergeant Kellin wondered how the sword could be brought up to the room unseen, and suddenly it occurred to me that it could have been concealed in the pipe brought up by the workman.'

'Go on,' the aide encouraged.

'Well, Sally stated that she could positively identify the man if she saw him again, and since I've been told that all the workmen in the city are registered with a trade guild, I presumed it would be a simple matter to find the man by going through the guilds. In fact, the sergeant agreed to take Sally to the headquarters of the plumbers' union first thing tomorrow morning to begin the search.' This last bit of information was news to Sergeant Kellin, who indeed faced me with a quizzical expression. But a sly wink of my eye bought his continued silence.

'Indeed,' Mr. Bullock said, his smile looking a bit forced. Turning to the sergeant, he added: 'And you are going to follow up on this lead?'

'I'm sure the mayor would expect as much from me,' Sergeant Kellin answered.

'Keep me informed of your progress.' Mr. Bullock then spun around and left the room.

Turning to me, the sergeant said: 'You never mentioned that the woman could identify the plumber.'

'That is because I just made it up,' I admitted. 'I was baiting the trap, and pray God it works.'

I was still silently praying some thirteen

hours later as John (who had spent most of the day happily giving interviews to the press about his years with Sherlock Holmes), Sergeant Kellin, three officers and I crouched uncomfortably in the darkness of Sally Probert's bedroom.

'Are you sure he will act tonight?' John asked.

'He has no choice,' I replied. 'If Sally is to be silenced before she can identify the workman, it has to be this evening.'

As though responding to a cue, footsteps were heard in the hallway outside, followed by the metallic scratching sound of the door lock being circumvented.

'Quiet, everyone,' Sergeant Kellin whispered as the outside door slowly creaked open. A large silhouetted figure made his way into the bedroom and stood over the prone figure in the bed. After a few breathless moments, a voice from the outer room called: 'Hurry up!'

'I can't do it,' the shadowy figure moaned. 'Not again.'

A second shadow then rushed into the bedroom and wrenched something from the other's hand. Raising the object high, the second man plunged it into the form on the bed.

'Now!' the sergeant shouted, and the policeman closest to the room light switched it on. Standing near the bed, a deadly Japanese dagger still clutched in his hand, stood Mr. Bullock, while the large man behind him looked on, terrified. Upon realizing he had been trapped, Bullock tore back the blankets on the bed to reveal a pile of pillows arranged in the form of a person.

'We thought it would be best if Sally Probert spent the night in another room,' I explained.

'I arrest you both for the murder of Constance Adams,' said Sergeant Kellin.

'He forced me to!' the large man suddenly blurted out.

'Shut up, Mordecai!' Bullock spat.

'To the devil with you, I won't!' He turned to address us. 'Bullock said she was an enemy of the party and standing in the way of its goals. He told me that if I helped him eliminate a thorn — that's what he called her, a thorn — I'd never have to worry about money again. But if I didn't help him, I'd be finished in the union — I'd never work again. I've got a family to support, and God help me, I did it.' The man sunk to his knees and started to weep.

Bullock regarded the weeping man with disgust, then met our eyes with defiance. 'I hope you are not expecting such base weakness from me. I regret nothing. The enemies of the Union Labour Party are to be stopped at all costs.'

'And the mayor,' Sergeant Kellin said, keeping a revolver trained on the killers, 'is he a part of this too?'

'That is the irony,' Bullock said, smiling bitterly. 'If Schmitz knew I was doing this, he would probably shoot me himself.'

More policemen arrived to take the weeping plumber and the crazed government official away, and once again, John and I returned to our hotel in a fair state of exhaustion.

Even so, I knew I could not put off the confrontation any longer. I had to know the truth. 'Before we retire, John, there is something we must discuss,' I said, opening my handbag and withdrawing the photograph, which I set down before him.

'Good Lord, where on earth did you get this?'

'It was delivered yesterday. Why have you never mentioned this before?'

'This? I suppose I felt it wasn't important enough.'

'Wasn't important enough?' I cried. 'Your first wedding?'

John stared at me, open-mouthed. 'My God, you're serious, aren't you?' he said finally. 'Oh, Amelia, is this why you have been acting so strangely towards me lately? Come and sit next to me and let me explain,' he entreated, and I did so.

'When I was barely out of school I accompanied a friend of mine named Jimson to America. We were two young lads thirsting for adventure and convinced we were going to find our fortunes in the gold country of California. Alas, we were about twenty years too late. We soon found ourselves stranded here with no money and few friends. Jimson wrote to his family, asking for money so we could return to England; but until it arrived we had to eat. We each found odd jobs. Mine you see here.'

'As someone's husband?'

'As a photographer's model. I had become acquainted with this photographer chap who for some reason thought that I looked like the perfect young husband. He also knew Constance, and he posed the two of us in costume and used the photo as an advertisement for his studio. After I returned home, Constance and I exchanged a friendly letter or two, but she was certainly not my wife.'

For the second time in as many days I was rendered speechless. When I finally found my voice, it was to utter: 'I am the stupidest creature on earth. How can you possibly love me?'

'It is quite easy, really,' he said, taking me in his arms.

The Adventure of the
Three Verners

Letter to Mrs. Elizabeth Newington
from Mrs. Amelia Watson
September 18, 1905

My dearest Beth —

I truly apologize for my complete silence these last several months. I assure you that I have not dropped off the edge of the earth, though once I relate to you the events that have transpired this past summer, you will perhaps understand why it has been so difficult for me to take up the pen.

It is no exaggeration to say that my world, if not the foundation of my very being, has been turned upside down and rent in a thousand pieces. Let me reassure you that this distress has not in any way been caused by John, who continues to be the same devoted and caring (if occasionally exasperating) man who stepped into my life two adventurous years ago.

233

Nor, oddly enough, has it been caused by Sherlock Holmes, whose presence in our lives has been mercifully sparse since Christmas, owing to his enthusiastic launch of a second career. I have been sworn to secrecy regarding his present activities, which are being carried out under an assumed name. Let me simply say that John's oft-stated belief that the theatre lost a great performer when Mr. Holmes chose to dedicate his life to detective work has proved quite astute.

This is not to say that Holmes has no bearing on the events that I am about to relate — for he has, even though he himself does not realize it. The true culprit in this matter, if there can be said to be a culprit, is my late father.

To start at the beginning, I am sure you recall that relations between my father and me were not always smooth. There were times when he could be a martinet of stunning proportions. You may remember his stubborn opposition to my being part of the amateur theatre, feeling it was not the sort of activity in which a proper young lady should be engaged. He at least tolerated my decision to become a governess, although he never let me forget that he felt the only role for women in society was as wife and mother.

(Have I ever told you of his last words? After he had suffered his final attack on the street, I rushed panic-stricken to the closest surgery I could find, which happened to be that of Dr. John H. Watson. We raced back to the place my father had fallen and upon seeing John, he looked up and uttered: 'Thank God, Amelia, you've found a man at last, and I approve of your choice,' then died. John, of course, did his best to comfort me, and you know the rest. But I digress.)

Father and I were never closer than during the last few years of his life, after I had moved in to take care of him. I am truly glad to have had those years. Even so, there always remained a fissure between us which, while dormant much of the time, became noticeably wide whenever I tried to speak of Mother. At the very mention of her name, Father became distant and uncommunicative, as though he still blamed me in some measure for her death. I knew I was not the only person in the world whose mother had died in childbirth, though my father had a knack for making it seem so. Or so I thought.

The train of events that caused the earth to spin backwards began on a day in early June, at which time John was once more absent, away in Cardiff regaling the Welsh with stories of his adventures with Sherlock Holmes. One day, as I was sorting through the meagre stack of post I had just received, I noticed an innocent-looking letter from a solicitor named Dennistoun Peale. Upon reading it, I learned that I had been summoned to the reading of the will of someone named Montague Verner, a name I had never heard in my life!

My first thought was that it was a mistake, and promptly dispatched a telegram to the solicitor informing him so. But the next day, I received a return telegram assuring me that there had been no error, and that all would be explained at the reading, which was to take place three days hence. If for no other reason than curiosity, I knew I must attend.

I arrived at the Tudor Street office of Mr. Peale at the appointed day and time to find that three others had preceded me. One was a woman of middle years who demonstrated a regal, if not haughty, demeanour. She was introduced as Hermione Verner, the widow of a Dr. Ralph Verner, who had been the only son of the deceased. The other two were the late Mr. Verner's niece and nephew. Douglas Verner, whom I judged to be roughly thirty years of age, was raven-dark and blessed with a rakish grin. His sister, Mrs. Caroline Erskine, appeared somewhat younger, though more care-worn. She was, I learned, the wife of a local shopkeeper. Despite her sombre appearance, she proved to be the most immediately outgoing of the three Verners.

'Did you know my late uncle?' Caroline asked me in a hushed, slightly hoarse voice, perhaps made so by the tightness of her high collar. I was forced to admit that I was as puzzled by my presence there as she. Mrs. Verner said nothing, though she continued to stare at me, as though trying to turn me to stone.

I was, in fact, still attempting to reason the situation out when Mr. Peale emerged from an inner office and entreated us to be seated around a long table. As we were taking our seats (the Verners all together on one side, myself on the other), the widow remarked, in a voice tinged with ice, 'The old man died nearly two months ago. Why did we have to wait so long for the will to be read?'

'There, there, Auntie,' Douglas Verner said, 'I'm sure Mr. Peale has his reasons.'

'Indeed I do, Mr. Verner,' the solicitor announced, taking a seat at the head of the table. The reason for the delay, according to Mr. Peale (whose lugubrious, plodding delivery would have put a hummingbird to sleep), was the result of a stunning deathbed declaration on the part of Montague Verner. 'It was believed, by me at least, that you three — Hermione, Douglas, Caroline — were his only living heirs,' the solicitor droned. 'However, his own testimony has revealed the existence of another.'

'Another?' Mrs. Verner questioned. Then, locking me in a frigid gaze, she added: 'Surely you cannot mean this creature.'

Rather than answer her uncivil challenge directly, Mr. Peale instead announced: 'Before I continue with the reading of the will, I would first like to read a letter written in my presence by Montague Verner, and entrusted to me mere hours before his death.' He carefully unfolded a sheaf of papers, spread them out before him, and with painful slowness donned a pair of spectacles. After clearing his throat, he read:

' 'Let no man think I am proud of what I am about to reveal. I cannot undo the damage that I have inflicted upon another human being as a result of my pride; though as I see the darkness approaching, I must do whatever I am able to make amends, however insignificant the effort may be. The parish record of St. Tristan's acknowledges the births of only three children to the Verner family within the past half-century: my son, Ralph, who has preceded me in death; and Douglas and

Caroline, the children of my sister Sophia. This, alas, is a lie.''

Here he paused dramatically, allowing us to absorb the pronouncement before continuing to read: ''There was a fourth child, a girl, born to my other sister, Rachel, who was not wed at the time. As scandalous as I considered that to be, and as great an affront to the good name of Verner, even I would not have sought for her the judgement that the Almighty Himself delivered for her sin: death, as the result of giving life to the child.''

As you can well imagine, Beth, my mind was beginning to reel at the implications of this deathbed confession.

The solicitor continued: ''My pride at the time would not allow me to acknowledge the child, yet neither could I bring myself to simply leave it as a foundling on the doorstep of the church. I confess that selfish interests in protecting the family name, coupled with genuine grief over my sister's sudden death, conspired to obscure my judgement. I therefore turned to a trusted friend, a man who had once saved my life in the thick of battle, Bertram Pettigrew — ''

At the mention of my father's name, my breathing all but stopped!

'' — and asked him for his advice as to what to do with the child. His answer both surprised and relieved me: *Give the child to me*, he said, *and no one will know*. I later learned that Major Pettigrew's wife had suffered the premature death of a child only some months before, a tragedy that continued to prey upon her mind until her own passing, barely a year later.''

How can I begin to describe, Beth, the feelings of confusion, puzzlement, and loss that were overwhelming me at that moment? If only John had been there to provide a comforting arm — a vain hope, I knew, since spouses are seldom welcomed in the readings of wills. As I struggled to think clearly in the face of such shock, I realized that the three Verners were eyeing me with expressions ranging from wonderment (chiefly Caroline) to outright horror (the widow).

''Pettigrew took the girl and raised her as his own,'' Mr. Peale continued, ''even after the death of his wife, at no time revealing to her that she was indeed an heir to the house of Verner. He went so far as to send me dispatches concerning her, though each of these I destroyed out of fear that someone else might stumble upon them and learn the family secret. As the decades passed, I remained secure in my belief that I had made the correct decision. Now, however, as I rapidly approach the Day of Judgement, I realize that my soul has been left wanting. With this testament, therefore, I am instructing my friend and solicitor, Mr. Dennistoun Peale, Esq., to use any means to discover the girl's whereabouts and, if she still be alive, attempt to make up for a lifetime of preterition. If these words are being heard by any of my heirs, it is an indication that he has completed this task.''

With that, Mr. Peale carefully refolded the pages, removed his glasses, gestured towards me and declared with great portent: 'I give you Amelia Pettigrew, now Mrs. John Watson, the long-lost daughter of Miss Rachel Verner, and niece and heir to Montague Verner.'

The widow's eyes narrowed. 'Do you mean to imply that we are expected to share our inheritance with her?' she asked coldly.

'That was the late Mr. Verner's wish,' the solicitor replied.

'She is our cousin, then?' Douglas asked, his grin now seeming quite forced.

Mr. Peale nodded.

'In that case, how do you do, cousin?' Caroline said.

'Honestly, I do not know,' I answered. 'Please understand I am quite taken aback and do not know what to think. I had no idea, none at all, that I was not the natural daughter of Bertram Pettigrew.'

While I was stammering unintelligently to my newfound cousins, Mrs. Verner was muttering: 'John Watson, why does that sound familiar? Something to do with Ralph, I daresay . . . '

She was quickly silenced by Mr. Peale's query: 'Would anyone like to hear the will itself?'

I will spare you all the legal skimble-skamble, Beth, and get straight to the heart of the matter. The three Verners were each remembered in the will with substantial amounts of money (apparently Montague Verner was a man of considerable means), which led me to believe that I was in line for the same. Try, then, to imagine my utter shock upon hearing that I was not to receive an equal share, but rather the bulk of the Verner estate, including a town house near Belgrave Square and a country home in Nottingham! My very breath seemed to evaporate in my lungs, leaving my entire body hollow and void. I tried to speak, but could not be heard over the objections of Mrs. Verner.

'You know very well that address in Belgravia belongs to me,' she informed the solicitor. 'Montague promised it to Ralph years ago.'

'Yes, Auntie, but Uncle Ralph is dead,' replied Douglas, who despite his veneer of calm seemed to be quite shaken.

'Which makes the property fully mine by law,' the widow declared victoriously.

Through it all, Caroline had remained silent, though curiously, each angry word from her aunt caused her to wince and raise a hand to her throat, which was obscured by the ruching of her high-collared shirtwaist. The gesture appeared to be unconscious.

'What evidence do we have that this woman is indeed who she claims to be?' Mrs. Verner was demanding.

'Actually, Mrs. Watson has not made any claim whatsoever,' Mr. Peale said. 'Rather, I am putting forth the claim on her behalf, based upon information that came as a result of a thorough investigation. Furthermore, permit me to point out that Mrs. Watson is a blood relative of Montague Verner, whereas you, Hermione, are related only through marriage.'

Believe me, Beth, when I say that the look Mrs. Verner gave the solicitor would have frozen fire itself. Mr. Peale, however, pretended not to notice. In fact, I sensed that he might actually be enjoying having the upper hand with the woman, if not enjoying her indignation.

At long last, Caroline Erskine spoke up. 'However shocked or distressed we are regarding this,' she said, 'Mrs. Watson must be more so. Perhaps, Aunt Hermione, we should let her come to terms with the situation before we attack her.'

'The shock is not simply from the inheritance,' I struggled to say, 'but also from learning that my father was not really my father, and that my mother . . .' Try as I might, I was unable to prevent the onrush of tears. I continued to battle the sobs, unsuccessfully, until Mr. Peale offered me the comfort of his private office until such time as I was able to compose myself. Thanking him, I rose and stepped to the door.

'I will come with you,' Caroline said, following me in and closing the door behind us. 'This must be incredibly difficult for you. May I call you Amelia?'

'Please do,' I said, finally managing to control my river of tears. 'And I trust I may call you Caroline.' Even as she smiled, I observed that her face was marked with some inner sadness.

'I hope you will not think too badly of Aunt Hermione,' she said. 'Since the death of Uncle Ralph, she has been out of sorts. I am sure she did not mean all of the rude things that she said.'

No, only a few of them, I thought, but said instead: 'Yes, I am sure my appearance here was quite a shock to her. I can only offer my apologies for inadvertently upsetting your family in such a time of sorrow.'

'Please don't apologize,' she said. 'I liked Uncle, but I cannot say I was close to him. In fact his bequeathal to me was more than I had expected.'

'What do you plan to do with the money, if I may ask?'

Her face clouded over and she unconsciously touched her throat again. 'Surely you realize that it will not be my money, but rather my husband's. That is the way things work.'

Examining her throat more closely, if discreetly, I thought I detected a trace of a purple mark underneath the white ruching. Perhaps it was a birthmark about which she was sensitive. 'Is anything the matter with your neck?' I ventured.

She looked startled. 'No, why?'

'I've noticed you touching it as though it was sore. If you need it examined, my husband is a doctor and — '

'No, I'm fine,' she interrupted, suddenly rising and turning away. I knew I had struck some kind of a nerve, but of what sort I was not yet certain.

Once I had fully recovered from my emotional outburst, Caroline and I returned to the outer office to discover that Mrs. Verner had already left. Mr. Peale began to make a vague apology for her behaviour, but I cut him short, asking: 'What would happen if I were to refuse the inheritance?'

'Refuse it?' the solicitor said. 'There is no reason you should refuse it, Mrs. Watson. However, if you were to do so, your share of the estate would be divided amongst the three remaining beneficiaries. I am familiar enough with the will Mr. Verner had filed prior to your inclusion as his heir, to distribute the assets in accordance with his wishes. If it is care of the property that concerns you, though, you would be far better off accepting the inheritance and then selling it to one of the other heirs.'

Douglas Verner's eyes brightened. 'I

would certainly be willing to entertain such an idea,' he chirped.

'Let me think it over this evening,' I said. 'I shall notify you tomorrow, Mr. Peale, regarding my intentions.'

With that, Beth, I left the office, and how grateful I was to get out! As I flagged a hansom, my mind still spinning, I wondered what the best course of action would be.

By that evening, I had made up my mind.

It was sometime after nine o'clock, as I was peacefully sitting and rereading *Nicholas Nickleby*, savouring each and every glorious contrivance of the plot, when the telephone jangled. Missy answered it and then summoned me.

'Someone from the solicitor's office, ma'am,' she said. Taking up the telephone, I heard a strange voice say: 'Mrs. Watson? My name is Caldwell. I'm an associate of Mr. Peale's and I'm afraid something has come up regarding the will. We need to see you at our offices at once.'

'At this hour?' I protested.

'I am sorry, madam, but it is rather urgent.'

'Oh, very well,' I said, then rang off. I informed Missy that I had been summoned to a lawyerly meeting, grabbed my jacket and hat and set out, arriving at Tudor Street some twenty minutes later. Immediately I noticed something suspicious: Mr. Peale's office was dark. If he and his associate were in there awaiting me, they were doing so without the benefit of light. My instincts told me to turn and run. If only I had listened to them.

As I continued to inspect the windows of the darkened office, I heard a voice call, 'Mrs. Watson? Over here.'

'Who is there?' I called back, seeing no one. Then a large figure silhouetted darkly against the night stepped out onto the walk. 'It's Caldwell, ma'am,' the figure said. 'Come with me.'

'I think not,' I told him, starting to back away.

In a matter of seconds, the man was upon me, holding me fast and forcing me into a pitch-dark alleyway next to the building. I felt a powerful hand tighten around my throat, all but blocking off my wind!

'Let ... me ... go!' I attempted to demand, though the words only came out as a hoarse creak.

'Not until I've had my say,' the brute replied, backing me up against the brick side of a building. There was not enough light to see his face, though I could feel his hot, onion-scented breath panting on me. Since his words had implied that his intention *was* to let me go, I ceased fighting.

'That's better,' he said. 'Now, you do as I tell you and you won't get hurt. Tomorrow you're going to tell that lawyer Peale that you intend to make no claim on that will. You understand? You are giving up your part of the inheritance lock, stock and barrel, or else.'

'Or else what?' I croaked.

Gripping my throat with extra force, which nearly propelled me into unconsciousness, he replied: 'Or else you might have to think about writing a will of your own.'

The man suddenly removed his hands from me and I sank down to the ground, coughing and wheezing. 'This is no idle threat, my girl,' he cautioned. 'I don't want to hear that you've accepted the estate.' A moment later he was gone, having disappeared into the darkness. I have no idea how long I remained in the dark alley before venturing out to hail another cab to take me home.

Once there, I'm afraid I alarmed poor Missy by staggering through the door and practically fainting on the floor. She raced to make tea for me, which burned as I drank it, but which ultimately soothed my aching throat.

'Who would do such a thing?' she demanded indignantly; and as I sipped, I tried to formulate an answer to that question in my own mind. The beast who attacked me was too large to be either Douglas Verner or Dennistoun Peale. Yet it had to be someone who knew about the will. Furthermore, his implied threat to me revealed that he was in a position to learn of my decision regarding the inheritance.

In an instant, I realized that there was only one person it could have been. My suspicions were further confirmed by the reflection that greeted me from my mirror as I prepared for bed.

The next morning, after carefully dressing, I set out for what was going to be a busy day. First I stopped at Mr. Peale's office to inform him of my intentions, and to obtain other information pertaining to my co-heirs. Next I travelled to Scotland Yard, where I asked to speak with Inspector Laurie, a CID officer whom I had come to know rather well. After a break for lunch, over which we discussed our plan of attack, the two of us made our way to a small furniture shop near Pall Mall.

Posing as disgruntled customers, we entered the store and demanded to see the owner, Mr. Colin Erskine, who quickly materialized from the back. Taking one look at me, he ushered us into his office. 'So, what can I do for you?' he asked, affecting an artificial smile that completely failed to disguise the cruel cut of his mouth.

'I have come to inform you that I will not accept the inheritance, Mr. Erskine,' I said, my voice still slightly hoarse from the previous night's attack on me. 'Or should I say, Mr. Caldwell?'

'I'm afraid I don't follow you,' he replied.

'I've no interest in playing games,' I fired back, angered by the wretch's devil-may-care attitude. 'I do not like your sort of game, anyway.' I loosened my collar to reveal the bruises on my neck, which were identical to the marks I had detected on the throat of his wife, Caroline, which she had worked so diligently to conceal. The thought of what other physical abuse he had subjected my young cousin to turned my stomach. 'Your hand made this mark, so do not bother denying it.'

He did not bother denying it. Instead he turned to Inspector Laurie, who had not as yet identified himself, and said, 'I suppose you're the husband, brought here to try and defend the lady's honour, is that it?'

'So you admit to attacking her?'

Inspector Laurie asked.

'I admit nothing,' Erskine replied, 'except that I could wring your neck, too, any day of the week, so don't get cocky with me, my friend. Now, is that all? I'm a busy man.'

'That is not all,' I said. 'I want you to understand that your attempt to choke the life out of me had nothing whatsoever to do with my decision. Montague Verner spent his entire life denying my existence, I am merely returning the favour and leaving his judgement to a higher court than I could possibly affect. What's more, I do not need a fortune in possessions and a town house in Belgravia. I am quite satisfied with my life as it is. Can you say that, Mr. Erskine?'

He was silent for a moment, then asked: 'Have you explained your decision to the lawyer?'

'I have.'

'Then good day.'

'Our business is not quite finished,' I went on. 'There is still the matter of your criminal assault on me.

'You can't touch me for that and you

255

know it,' he sneered.

'Perhaps I could,' Inspector Laurie said, flashing his identification under the nose of the stunned Erskine.

'I thought you were her husband!' Erskine cried.

'I am Mrs. Watson's friend,' the inspector replied. 'Would you still like to try and wring my neck?'

The merchant's face went pale. 'What are you going to do?'

'Were it up to me, you would already be incarcerated,' Inspector Laurie said. 'However, Mrs. Watson has told me that she has no intention to press charges.'

'I appreciate it, ma'am,' Mr. Erskine said. Now it was *ma'am*!

'You are not welcome, I assure you,' I replied, 'and my willingness to let the matter drop rests entirely on one condition: that you never lay a filthy hand on my cousin Caroline as long as you live. Like it or not, Mr. Erskine, I am now part of your wife's family, and if I ever see a mark on her again, or even so much as hear that you have touched her, I will not hesitate to call on Inspector Laurie.'

'And it will be my pleasure to show you how accommodating our fine London gaols can be,' the inspector added.

'Now we have finished,' I said, and without another word, I turned and marched out of the shop, followed by Inspector Laurie.

John returned home a fortnight later, by which time, thank heavens, the bruises on my neck had vanished. So had a large portion of my belated anger at my 'father' for having died without first breaking the truth to me himself. I decided not to inform John of the events that had sent my mind and soul reeling, and that vow I have kept.

Heavens, Beth, but this is a long letter! Perhaps I should turn it into a book and publish it. But the tale is not quite over yet. Please bear with me a little while longer as I tell you of the unexpected, almost unbelievable finale to this affair. And if you are not sitting down already, you may want to.

With John back home, our lives returned to normal (more or less), and remained that way until a little over a week ago. We had just returned from an evening of the theatre when he blurted: 'Amelia, what would you think if I proposed to retire from my medical practice?'

Needless to say, I was quite startled by the suddenness of it. 'Heavens, dear, what would you do with yourself?' I asked him.

'I believe I could write and lecture full-time,' he said, his eyes positively dancing with enthusiasm. 'You know I have been getting more and more requests for speaking engagements, and I have also been thinking about tackling a full-length play centring on my exploits with Holmes. What do you think?'

I didn't quite know what to think, and told him so, after which I innocently asked what he planned to do with his practice, which had been increasing as a result of his growing celebrity.

'Sell it, of course,' he replied. 'What a pity that Dr. Verner is dead. He could buy it from me again.'

Had I heard right? 'Did you say *Verner*, dear?' I asked, trying to sound casual.

'Indeed. A chap named Ralph Verner bought my old practice in Kensington some years back, while I was still living with Mary.'

My jaw dropped as I finally comprehended the reason Mrs. Verner thought she recognized the name John Watson.

'The curious thing was,' he went on, 'some time afterwards I learned that Holmes had actually put up a portion of the money for him.'

'Mr. Holmes helped to purchase your practice? Why on earth did he do that?'

'It seems that Dr. Verner was a distant relative of his. I suppose it proves that blood really is thicker than water, even for someone like Holmes.'

I have, of course, never been struck by a moving train, though the realization of what John had just confided in me was probably as close as I shall come to the experience.

'A distant relative of *Sherlock Holmes*?' I cried.

'Yes, they are all descended from a French painter named Vernet.'

At that moment, Beth, to my eternal

shame, I fainted away like the witless heroine of a penny dreadful. The next thing I remember was John reviving me with foul-smelling salts. 'I had no idea you would take it this way, Amelia. Forgive me,' he pleaded. 'I will not sell the practice if my keeping it means that much to you!'

How could I explain to him, Beth, that the reason for my faint was not his desire to retire, but the almost inconceivable discovery that *I was a blood relation to Sherlock Holmes*? Once I recovered from my swoon and the shock that accompanied it, however, I began to laugh. Before long I was reduced to such a state of helpless hysteria that John grew worried and prepared a draught for me.

So, my dear Beth, I now confide in you this privileged information. I have no intention of ever informing John or 'cousin Sherlock' of my discovery (perhaps secrecy is a Verner family trait). Some days back, however, for reasons I still cannot precisely explain, I was suddenly consumed with the need to tell *somebody*. I found myself signalling the telephone exchange operator for a private number in Whitehall. After an unearthly number of rings, a familiar voice answered curtly, 'Holmes.'

'Mr. Holmes, this is Amelia Watson.'

'How are you, madam?' crowed Mycroft Holmes, Sherlock's elder (and slightly more personable) brother, who is a vital member of His Majesty's Government (*how* vital I care not to disclose). 'What can I do for you?'

Taking a deep breath, I related the entire story of the three Verners, and awaited his response. After what seemed like an hour of silence, he intoned: 'Welcome to the family, my dear. Permit me to quote you a price, should you ever wish to buy your way out.'

I laughed to the point of embarrassment, and then cut off the line.

As the result of opening a letter from an unknown solicitor, I have acquired a new aunt, who is quite horrid; a new male cousin, who on most days seems as indifferent as cooked rice; a new female cousin, who is already becoming a dear friend (never to replace you, of course,

Beth), even though she is married to a reprehensible lout; a once-respectable husband who now harbours a desire to write and produce melodramas for the theatre; and two distant relations who happen to be the most idiosyncratic men I have ever encountered in my life.

There are times, Beth, when I have awakened at night, wondering if I should pursue Mycroft Holmes's offer to buy my way out of the family. Having already given up a sizeable inheritance, however, I would more than likely have to take up a collection to raise the necessary amount.

May I put you down for a pound?

Yours ever,

Amelia